FORBIDDEN FEAST

BOOK THREE OF THE ETERNAL DEAD SERIES

ALSO BY ALLISON HOBBS
Brick
Scandalicious
Put a Ring On It
Lipstick Hustla
Stealing Candy
The Sorceress
Pure Paradise
Disciplined
One Taste
Big Juicy Lips
The Climax
A Bona Fide Gold Digger
The Enchantress
Double Dippin'
Dangerously in Love
Insatiable
Pandora's Box

WRITING AS JOELLE STERLING
The Dark Hunger
Midnight Cravings

Joelle Sterling

FORBIDDEN FEAST

BOOK THREE OF THE ETERNAL DEAD SERIES

STREBOR BOOKS

NEW YORK LONDON TORONTO SYDNEY

Strebor Books
P.O. Box 6505
Largo, MD 20792
http://www.streborbooks.com

ISBN 978-1-59309-493-5
ISBN 978-1-4767-0579-8 (ebook)
LCCN 2012951716

First Strebor Books trade paperback edition April 2013

Cover design: www.mariondesigns.com
Cover photograph: © Keith Saunders/Marion Designs

10 9 8 7 6 5 4 3 2 1

Manufactured in the United States of America

For information regarding special discounts for bulk purchases,
please contact Simon & Schuster Special Sales at 1-866-506-1949
or business@simonandschuster.com

The Simon & Schuster Speakers Bureau can bring authors to your live event.
For more information or to book an event, contact the Simon & Schuster Speakers
Bureau at 1-866-248-3049 or visit our website at www.simonspeakers.com.

For my niece, Imani Perry

CHAPTER 1

Holland Manning peered at the screen of her phone, wishing Jonas would contact her. Disheartened, she tossed the phone in her purse and sighed as she observed the swarm of students that clogged the school's corridors. Getting through her first day back at Frombleton High wasn't going to be easy. For the first time in her life, Holland wanted to go unnoticed. But, as luck would have it, kids were staring at her, as if she were an exchange student from another planet.

Unfortunately, Holland had to squeeze through a crowd of gawking, smart-mouthed boys as she searched for her locker.

"Check out Holland Manning? When did she get hot?" a giggling sophomore asked in a voice loud enough for Holland to hear.

"I hear Botox works wonders…or maybe she got a nose job! Whatever she had done is totally working," replied another obnoxious boy.

Holland's face flushed with embarrassment as she navigated through the mob of students. When she finally located her locker, she spotted Chaela Vasquez from the corner of her eye. Chaela was flanked by Paige Holbrook and Elle Schmidt, and Holland's heart sank as the three cheerleaders glided in her direction. She simply didn't have the emotional strength to exchange insults with Chaela and her two snotty friends. Hoping the girls would pass her by without any catty comments, Holland avoided their gazes and pretended to be engrossed in opening her combination lock.

"Look who's back in town," Elle said with undisguised disdain.

"And she's all glammed up with a new hairdo," Paige added snidely.

"She tried to steal Jarrett, and now she probably wants to sink her claws into Chaela's new boyfriend." Elle spoke in a high volume, designed to pique the curiosity of the other students that meandered through the halls.

A small crowd began to gather, and Holland felt compelled to stand up for herself. Whirling around, she faced the three mean girls. Elle and Paige glared at her, while Chaela looked downward, unwilling to meet Holland's gaze.

"Chaela!" Holland said sharply, forcing Chaela to glance up and look her in the eye. "I never tried to steal Jarrett from you. He lied and told me that you two broke up," Holland explained.

"It doesn't matter; it's cool," Chaela mumbled and anxiously chewed on a fingernail.

"No, it's not cool," Paige disagreed, her face twisted in repugnance. "You caught her cheating with Jarrett and you're gonna let her get away with it?"

Grinning and jeering, a few overly zealous students began to chant, "Girl fight! Girl fight!"

"I don't have a problem with Holland. Jarrett's the past, and I've moved on," Chaela explained, sounding uncharacteristically reasonable. She glanced at Holland. "Listen, you can have Jarrett if you want; he's all yours."

"No thanks; I have a boyfriend," Holland replied calmly.

Unlike her typical, confident self, Chaela seemed frazzled and her eyes shifted around anxiously. Holland also noticed that Chaela didn't look as polished or as put together as usual. There were dark circles around her eyes, like she hadn't slept in days. Her nail polish was chipped, and the nail on her left index finger had been nibbled down to the quick. Her hair was pulled back into a messy ponytail, and there were errant wisps of hair that she kept pushing out of her face. Holland had never seen Chaela look so terrible. She was completely disheveled in a wrinkly, uncoordinated outfit with colors that clashed.

Displeased with the civil exchange of words between Chaela and Holland, Elle's dark eyes glinted with malevolence. "Chaela's dating the hot, quarterback from Willow Hills, and so, you can have creepy Jarrett Sloan. You two losers deserve each other," she said spitefully.

"I'm not interested in Jarrett," Holland said in exasperation. Then, bitterly recalling how the three cheerleaders used to terrorize her friend, Naomi, Holland suddenly became hot with anger. She advanced toward them so abruptly and in such a threatening manner, the girls flinched and took several steps backward.

"If you girls are looking for someone to bully, you chose the wrong person. I'm not tolerating it. Do you understand?" Holland said in a raised voice.

"Whoa! Holland Manning is gonna kick some cheerleader butt," an onlooker yelled, hoping to instigate a fight.

"Lighten up, Holland. We were only kidding." Elle giggled nervously.

Keeping her eyes downcast, Chaela muttered, "Let's go; we're gonna be late for class." Flinging their hair, Elle and Paige sashayed along the corridor. Walking between them, Chaela kept her head hung low.

With no brawl to witness, the group of spectators muttered in disappointment as they reluctantly dispersed.

Doreen Johnson emerged from the throng of students and sidled up to Holland. "Way to go, Holland. I bet the bitch squad won't be bothering you anymore."

"Probably not," Holland said with indifference.

"Where've you been? Heard you were at some fancy-schmancy school."

"Yeah, I was away at boarding school."

"What happened…did you get kicked out?"

"No. I left on my own. Got homesick." Holland gave a tight smile and then closed her locker. "See you later; I have to get to my homeroom before the bell."

"Who do you have for homeroom?" Doreen asked.

"Mr. Haroldson."

"I have Haroldson, too." Doreen fell into step with Holland. "You should have stayed as far away from Frombleton as possible."

"Why?"

"Crazy shit's been happening. Didn't you hear about Doug Shriver?"

"Yeah, I heard a rumor."

"It's more than a rumor. Doug claims he was bitten by a gang of vampires." Doreen peered at Holland, waiting for her reaction.

"A *gang* of vampires?"

"Uh-huh. Teenage vampires," Doreen added. "The McFadden woman said the same thing…she said that she and her husband were abducted by two normal-looking teens who turned out to be vicious vampires. She claims her husband was bled dry by a pack of them. People aren't taking these cases seriously; they don't want to believe that vampires actually exist."

Holland knew all too well that the bloodsuckers existed. A shiver rippled through her as she recalled her battle with the Sullivan family. Thankfully, her blood was lethal to vampires, but she wasn't sure if she could survive an attack by a gang of them.

Doreen paused outside of Mr. Haroldson's class. She reached inside her stretchy pink top and furtively revealed a silver crucifix. "I'm wearing this for protection," she whispered. "You should get one, too; I heard that the vamps are planning to take over Frombleton."

"Where're you getting your information?"

"A friend of mine hangs with the vamps."

The girls entered the classroom and Holland took a vacant seat next to Doreen. "Your friend is probably making up the story; putting a spin on the rumors that are circulating," Holland suggested, fishing for more information about the vampires.

"It's true. Vamps are right here in Frombleton. I used to go to their parties, too. But now that…" Doreen paused and swallowed. "Now that they're…you know…murdering people, I've been steering clear of them. But my friend is still partying with them. And, um, so is Jarrett Sloan," she said in a voice that was low and confidential.

"Jarrett's hanging with vamps!" Holland exclaimed.

"Keep your voice down," Doreen cautioned.

"Sorry," Holland murmured. Last summer, after being a blood slave for Zac the vampire, Jarrett had barely escaped with his life intact. *Why would he want to hang out with a vampire gang?* Holland mused.

"Knowing what the vampires are up to has been eating at me. I couldn't risk sounding like a lunatic, so I haven't talked about this with anyone…" Doreen went quiet and she looked around suspiciously. "Other than my friend, I haven't talked about the vamps with anyone until now."

"Why'd you decide to tell me?"

"I don't know; I guess you seemed weird enough to believe me." Doreen gave an apologetic smile.

Holland didn't wince at the back-handed compliment. She no longer cared what anyone thought of her. And to be honest, being a witch of the First Order definitely qualified her as a weirdo.

"Who is this mysterious friend of yours? And why isn't she worried about vamps taking over the town?"

"She's actually my ex-best friend. She stole my vamp boyfriend—a hot dude named Chaos. Chaos can be an egotistical dick, but he's so sexy, it's easy to overlook his flaws," Doreen said dreamily.

"Wow, your best friend stole your boyfriend?"

"It may not be her fault...vampires can do mind control, you know. I mean, it was so unexpected for her to start dating Chaos. She was seeing several vampire dudes, and she used to criticize me for being so emotionally invested in Chaos. You can't imagine how hurt and shocked I was when she suddenly fell head over heels in love with him. She actually bragged about how much she likes it when he sucks her blood until she passes out."

Holland grimaced. "Why would she let him do that?"

"The rush. It's exciting and intense; like sexual asphyxiation, I guess."

Holland didn't know anything about sexual asphyxiation, but she did know that fooling around with vamps was life-threatening! Naomi had been infatuated with a vampire, and it turned out badly. It was chilling to think that another classmate was romantically involved with a dangerous bloodsucker.

"My friend, uh, Sophia...she hasn't been to school in three days. My calls go straight to voice mail. And even though she's a backstabbing, massive A-hole, I'm still worried about her. I stopped by her house after school yesterday, and her dad's car is in the driveway, but nobody's home. It's like the entire household has disappeared."

Sophia Stoddard! Holland recalled that Sophia and Doreen were close friends. During middle school, Sophia had acquired a reputation for being…well, sort of loose.

Doreen bit her bottom lip. "I think I know where Sophia's family is."

"Where?"

"Downtown. At the old Lilac Hotel."

Holland stared blankly at Doreen for a moment. "That old, abandoned hotel?"

Doreen nodded. "That's the vampires' hideout. It's where they sleep during the day."

"How many?"

"Lots of 'em. A couple dozen live there, and Chaos and a few others visit often."

So, the old Lilac Hotel is their nest! Holland couldn't stifle a smile. Once she passed this information on to Rebecca Pullman, the vampire crisis would be over. The residents of Frombleton would be safe, and the force field around her house could be removed, and she and her mom would no longer be on lockdown after dark.

CHAPTER 2

"Let's stop here," Eden said, pointing to Leroy's Place, a quaint little grocery store about seventy miles outside of Willow Hills. "Seems peaceful. I doubt if the biters have made it this far."

Expressionless, Gabe nodded as he slowed the Explorer and pulled into the dirt lot. There was an iridescent blue Mercedes in the parking lot that sparkled in the sunlight. The flashiness of the car was a complete contrast to the down-home appearance of the place.

With its white clapboard exterior, a pink and blue neon clock in the window, a red wooden screen door, a pair of rocking chairs on the porch, and a big green banner that read: *Homemade Sandwiches*, the store had the historic charm of old Americana.

"Looks pretty inviting," Eden observed optimistically.

"Mmm-hmm," Gabe murmured without interest.

"I could go for a homemade sandwich…can't remember the last time I ate anything substantial. I'm suddenly starving…what about you?"

"Nah, I don't have an appetite."

"We have a long trip ahead of us; you have to put something in your stomach."

Irritation flashed in Gabe's eyes. "Look, I said I'm not hungry! Now, let's get whatever we need and get back on the road!"

"Sure, okay," Eden said, realizing how inconsiderate it was of her to try and coerce Gabe into a better mood. He was grieving over his grandmother and she'd simply have to accept his gloomy disposition.

"Hey, I'm sorry I yelled at you," Gabe said as he turned off the ignition. "You're right; I should try to eat something."

Without a word, Eden patted Gabe's hand.

Cradling little Jane Doe in her arms, Eden took in the tranquil atmosphere. On the left-hand side of the store was a tall peach tree and a sturdy sycamore. The picnic tables that were off to the right were shaded by a massive weeping willow. The side of the building closest to the parking lot was decorated with an over-sized, red Coca-Cola bottle cap and several large wooden placards that advertised products from a bygone era.

Confident that the biters were confined to Willow Hills—at least for the time being—Eden looked down at Jane and cooed, "It's a long drive to New York, and we've got to load up on formula and diapers for you."

"And some grub for us," Gabe threw in with a chuckle, but the raw pain of losing his grandmother was evident in his eyes. "Oh, yeah, we're getting low on gas. I guess we're gonna have to fill up before we get back on the highway." He pointed to a BP gas station sign that towered in the distance.

The moment they opened the red screen door, they could smell the wonderful aromas that wafted through the store. Leroy's Place offered a serene atmosphere, and it seemed that Eden and Gabe had walked into an era when life was uncomplicated and simple.

"Awesome," Gabe gushed, nodding to the throwback glass candy case filled with old classics like Candy Cigarettes, Squirrel Nuts, BB Bats, and Sugar Daddy Pops. "I'm getting a sugar rush just looking at this stuff."

A few feet from the candy case, a portly man with thick and bristling eyebrows and thinning white hair wore plastic gloves as he made sandwiches for a stylish couple.

"Howdy," he welcomed Gabe and Eden. "Welcome to Leroy's where you'll find the best dang sandwiches in the state of Georgia," he boasted.

"He's right," confirmed the well-dressed woman. Her hair was fixed in a perfectly coiffed topknot. She was wearing a pencil skirt, leopard-print top, black satin pumps, and an impressive diamond on her ring finger. Her equally attractive male companion had on tailored pants, and he wore a vest and tie over a crisp white shirt. His shirt sleeves, Eden noticed, were neatly folded at the elbows. The classy couple looked out of place in the quaint grocery store; they seemed like the types that would be more comfortable dining in an elegant restaurant. *That shiny Mercedes has to belong to them*, Eden concluded.

"First time here?" the woman asked. Gabe and Eden both nodded. "Well, be careful or you'll end up like me and my fiancé, Chuck. Leroy's sandwiches are so addictive, we drive over twenty miles, twice a week—just to taste his amazing sandwiches."

Leroy tossed Gabe and Eden another proud smile. "Look at the menu and I'll be with you in a second."

Gabe's eyes shifted upward to the list of sandwiches that were posted on the wall, and Eden grabbed a miniature shopping cart and began browsing the aisles, searching for items the baby would need. Eyes squinted, she scanned the shelves checking for the same brand of formula that Jane was already drinking.

The well-dressed woman joined her in the aisle. "You're lucky, you know," she said, smiling.

Eden looked up, her brows furrowed in curiosity.

"You're lucky to have missed the lunch crowd." She peered down at her expensive-looking watch. "This place is packed during the lunch rush, but it's pretty relaxed at supper time." She walked toward Eden, her eyes glistening with joy. "I love babies. Boy or girl?"

"Girl. Her name's Jane." Eden shifted Jane in her arms, allowing the woman to see her face.

"Oh, she's adorable. Such a precious little jewel," she remarked, stroking Jane's cheek.

"Charlotte! Come on, babe. I've got your pimento cheese spread sandwich," Chuck called out with a trace of impatience in his voice.

"Did you get the garlic habanero mayonnaise on the side?" Charlotte said from the baby products aisle.

"Yeah, and a tall glass of sweet tea."

"Be right out," Charlotte replied.

After the sounds of the screen door squeaking open and then slamming closed, Charlotte held out her arms. "Can I hold the baby? Chuck and I are getting married next year, but we agreed to hold off on kids for another five years." A pained look crossed Charlotte's face. "I agreed, but in my heart of hearts, I want a baby so bad, I can taste it."

Eden carefully placed Jane in Charlotte's arms. Chuck and Charlotte appeared to be the kind of people that could give Jane a decent home. Too bad they wouldn't be ready for a family for another five years, and too bad they lived so close to Willow Hills. Even if they were interested in raising Jane, Eden couldn't leave Jane with a couple that lived within a fifty-mile radius of the ravenous biters that roamed the area.

Charlotte returned Jane to Eden's arms. "We're eating outside in the picnic area. Why don't you and your husband and your adorable baby join us when you get your food."

"Oh, Jane's not my— Uh, sure, we'll join you," Eden said, catching herself from admitting she wasn't Jane's mother.

Divulging that information could lead to all sorts of trouble. She wanted to warn Charlotte, Chuck, and the kindly sandwich maker about the biters. But how could she do that without sounding completely insane? Eden gnawed at her bottom lip, trying to figure out a way to bring up the subject.

"What'll it be, lil' lady?" Leroy asked when Eden emerged from the aisle pushing the small cart that was exploding with baby supplies.

She gazed at the menu. "I'll try the ham and Swiss cheese on potato bread."

"Good choice," Leroy said. "Lettuce, red onion, tomatoes, and avocado?"

"Umm..."

"Oh, live dangerously," Leroy encouraged with a twinkle in his eyes. "The extras come with the price of the sandwich."

"Okay, pile it all on," Eden said with a smile. Leroy was putting her at ease and it felt good to relax for a bit.

Letting his guard down somewhat and seeming to enjoy the charming atmosphere of Leroy's Place, Gabe smiled, too. "I'll have the peanut butter and jelly with sliced bananas on regular, white bread."

Leroy entertained them with jokes as he prepared their sandwiches. Gabe laughed heartily and Eden was warmed by the sound of his laughter. They both needed this brief encounter with normal folks.

"Want me to wrap these...to go? Or are you grabbing a table outside?" Leroy asked.

"We're eating outside," Eden said. Gabe gave her a quizzical look. "I told Charlotte we'd join her and Chuck," she explained.

Gabe shrugged but Eden could see a fleeting glimpse of annoyance in his eyes. He wanted to hit the road and put a lot more distance between them and the biters, but she wanted to enjoy a few more moments of the little paradise they'd stumbled upon. Furthermore, she wanted to warn Charlotte and Chuck about the rampant, biting disease that had taken over Willow Hills. Caution them to steer clear of the area. They could pass the information on to Leroy, and he could spread the word to all his customers.

Eden left the shopping cart parked close to the counter. "I have to pick up a few more items after we eat," she explained to Leroy.

Leroy nodded. "Take your time and enjoy the sandwiches."

Eden carried Jane, and Gabe carried the tray with their sandwiches and soft drinks to the picnic area. Out of Leroy's earshot, Gabe whispered harshly, "We don't have time for a double date with those two phonies."

"Charlotte seems very nice."

"Chuck is arrogant, and I don't like him," Gabe grumbled.

"Well, I figured we'd use the opportunity to tell them what's going on."

"They're gonna think we're crazy."

"Probably, but I'll feel better knowing that we warned them."

Gabe and Eden sat across from the stylish couple, and Charlotte smiled in delight. Chuck, on the other hand, gave a little groan and scowled down at his watch.

Eden placed the baby across her lap and picked up her sandwich. "Mmm. Delicious," she murmured after she bit into it.

"I told you…Leroy's sandwiches are to die for," Charlotte said.

Accepting that they had nothing in common, Gabe and Chuck chewed their food and ignored each other.

"How old is the baby?" Charlotte wanted to know.

"A few months. Uh, she's actually not ours. We're babysitting Jane."

"What a relief," Charlotte blurted. "You two seem far too young for the responsibility of taking care of child. Now Chuck and I… we're financially secure, but we're putting off parenting until…" She glanced at Chuck. "What exactly are we waiting for, sweetheart?"

"We're waiting until we're ready to devote all of our free time to changing diapers and singing lullabies." Chuck wiped his hands with a napkin, gave a tight smile, and stood. "Nice meeting you two," he said to Eden and Gabe. "Let's go, Charlotte. I have to see a client in an hour; we'd better get moving if we plan on beating traffic."

A quick look of yearning swept over Charlotte's face. "Can I hold the baby one more time?"

Chuck groaned and rolled his eyes.

"Sure." Eden lifted Jane from her lap and Charlotte hurried to the other side of the wooden table.

As Charlotte rocked Jane and made cooing sounds, a dark-colored Prius sped down the road with its tires squealing.

"Here comes the supper crowd. We have to go, Charlotte," Chuck said firmly.

The Prius peeled through the parking lot, but instead of stopping to park, it careened out of control, zigzagging across the lawn, and finally slamming into the sycamore tree.

Charlotte let out a shocked cry. Jane wailed and squirmed at the sound of the collision. Eden took Jane from Charlotte's arms, and comforted her.

Charlotte shot a frantic look at Chuck. "Call the paramedics!"

Looking aggravated by the inconvenience of having to help out, Chuck sighed and then grudgingly pulled out his cell.

Leroy ran out of the store. "What the…?" Wide-eyed, he stared at the crashed Prius. The windshield had a circular crack, the driver's side door was caved in, and the front end of the car was jammed into the trunk of the tree. Leroy began frantically waving to Chuck and Gabe. "Help me over here, fellas!"

"Get away from the car," Gabe yelled as he cautiously approached.

"Are you nuts? Someone may be injured." Leroy peered through the window. "There's a man inside; he has a gash in his head. There's a lot of blood; that fella's banged up real good." Leroy anxiously tugged on the door handle. Unable to get it open, he scurried around to the passenger's side.

Gabe lunged for Leroy, practically tackling him away from the car. "I'm serious; you can't open that door. The person inside could be infected."

Charlotte scowled at Eden, her eyes stretched wide and questioning. "Infected? What's your boyfriend talking about?"

"He's not my boyfriend. We're just friends."

"Whatever! What kind of infection is he talking about?"

"A virus or something. It started in Willow Hills. Some people think there's a rabies outbreak, but whatever it is, it makes people act violent…and they bite."

"They bite!" Charlotte repeated with a look of disbelief.

Eden nodded grimly.

Leroy tore himself from Gabe's grasp. "Get your hands off of me; there's an injured man in that car and you're acting like a lunatic." Leroy jiggled the door handle, but it was locked. Appealing to Chuck, he called out, "Hey, buddy, the guy in the car is bleeding badly; we've got to get him out of there. Will you give me a hand?"

Chuck sighed and frowned as he paced toward the wreck. "I have to meet a client soon, and I can't show up with blood stains on my clothes." He paused and regarded the wreckage. "Look, I called an ambulance, and I think we should let the professionals handle this."

"What's wrong, afraid to get a little blood on your prissy white shirt?" Leroy scoffed. "This is a matter of life and death and I'll be dang if I'm gonna stand by and watch a man bleed out!" No longer wearing his friendly, sandwich-maker smile, Leroy muttered profanities as he stormed to the garage behind the picnic area.

Gabe peered through the car window. The man's mouth and eyes were wide open in death. When Leroy came running out of the garage with a crowbar in hand, Gabe held out a hand in warning. "Don't open that door. The man is already dead and he's probably infected," Gabe shouted, but Leroy pushed past him. Giving up on convincing Leroy that the driver of the car could be dangerous, Gabe made long strides toward the picnic area. "Let's go, Eden. I told you no one would listen. Let's go; we're outta here."

Eden turned in the direction of the Explorer and then whirled around. "Wait! The diapers and formula are inside, in the shopping cart."

"I'll get 'em. Take the baby and wait for me in the truck." Gabe raced past the collision. Leroy seemed to be a good person, and he couldn't help feeling pity as he witnessed the man panting and working up a sweat as he struggled to pry open the car door.

Inside the store, Gabe went behind the counter and found piles of shopping bags. He unloaded the items from the cart and packed them inside the bags. Estimating the total for their meal and the baby products, he tossed three twenties on the counter. Outside, he rushed past Leroy, shouting, "The money's on the counter."

Leroy grunted in disgust and continued trying to jimmy open the door.

Running to the parking lot, Gabe noticed Chuck guiding Charlotte toward the Mercedes. *Smart move.* If a biter had managed to sink its teeth into the unfortunate driver, as Gabe suspected, then Leroy was going to find himself in a world of trouble.

CHAPTER 3

Traveling slowly but erratically, another car—a Buick—inched toward Leroy's Place. The driver's door was partially open as the vehicle crawled along. The car came to a stop in the middle of the road. The door opened wider and a woman's tanned legs came into view. Then, the rest of her body spilled out, revealing a pink dress that was stained with blood. Groaning miserably, she slid to the ground.

Briefly immobilized by the dreadful sight of the injured woman, Leroy suspended his efforts in trying to help the man in the Prius. Holding the crowbar limply at his side, he gaped in disbelief. "What in God's name is going on?" Leroy wondered aloud. Gathering his wits, he dropped the crowbar and raced to the road to assist the second bloodied victim.

Behind the wheel of the Mercedes, Chuck tore out of the lot and whizzed past the incapacitated woman without giving her a second glance.

Gabe cruised up to the Buick, stuck his head out the window and yelled at Leroy, "Don't go near her, man. I'm serious. Get inside your store and lock the door!"

"You don't understand what you're dealing with; these people have a deadly disease," Eden added frantically.

Refusing to heed the warnings, Leroy bent over the second victim, grimacing as he examined her injuries. "How did she get these deep gouges all over her body? How the heck could something like this happen?"

"Leroy, you have to listen to us. That woman is infected and it's only a matter of time before she turns," Eden said urgently.

"I'm not listening to that crap you're saying. You two are bonkers." Leroy waved a dismissive hand. "What's taking that ambulance so long? This woman is going to bleed to death if she doesn't get help. Looks like she's been mauled within an inch of her life." He pulled off his apron and hurriedly wrapped it around the oozing wound on the woman's shoulder. "Give me a hand over here," Leroy yelled at Gabe. "How can you sit there and watch this poor lady suffer?"

"There's nothing you can do for her. Your best bet is to lock yourself inside your store before these folks start turning."

"Turning into what? Have you been smoking dope?" Leroy scoffed.

Suddenly there was the unmistakable sound of a car crash, and Leroy jumped to his feet. Rubbing his head in befuddlement, he stared southward and exclaimed, "God, Almighty! A truck just plowed into the Mercedes—down by the BP station."

Chill bumps rose on Eden's arms and her heart beat wildly. She shot a terrified look at Gabe. "We have to take a different route to the highway," Gabe said, shifting gears and then backing up a little. "Hopefully, we'll find another filling station on the way."

Eden clutched his arm. "Wait, Gabe. Shouldn't we try to help Charlotte and Chuck? We can't let the biters get them. And Leroy—we can't leave him defenseless, either."

Shielding his eyes from the sun, Gabe gazed in the direction that the Mercedes had driven and then glanced at Leroy. "It's probably too late for Charlotte and Chuck. And Leroy's too stubborn to listen. I can't make him believe us. What do you want me to do—force him to come with us at gunpoint?"

Eden looked out her window. The woman on the ground was lying still now, and Leroy was losing it, hysterically yelling for help as he ripped off his shirt, using it along with his apron to try and staunch the bleeding.

"Oh, no!" Gabe blurted and Eden jerked around, following Gabe's line of vision. Limping and barefoot, her pencil skirt torn, Charlotte sobbed loudly as she hobbled forward. Her topknot had come undone and her hair was tangled around her shoulders.

"They got Chuck," Charlotte wailed. "A bunch of crazy people got him." She pointed behind her. "They were like wild animals…ripping, tearing, and biting Chuck!"

"What are you talking about?" Abandoning the woman on the ground, Leroy rushed to Charlotte. "What crazy people?"

"They're down by the gas station. And they're all nuts; you can't reason with them. A truck crashed into us, and our airbags exploded. A small crowd of people gathered around the car and started pulling Chuck out. I thought they were trying to help us…until I noticed how roughly they were tugging on Chuck. And then they started growling, clawing, and biting him. They were actually *biting* him!" Charlotte repeated, her voice escalating to a shriek.

Leroy cast a scathing look at Gabe and Eden. "All hell is breaking out, and you two are sitting nice and cozy inside your truck and doing nothing to help."

"There's nothing we can do. That woman you're trying to help was attacked by the same *things* that attacked Charlotte and Chuck. You'd be wise to keep your distance from her. They change after they've been bitten."

"Change into what?" Leroy asked, his face twisted in disgust.

"Into biters," Eden murmured, rocking Jane in her arms. "The infection started in Willow Hills, and we thought it was safe to stop here, but obviously we were wrong."

Gabe nodded. "Those biters are multiplying faster than we anticipated. We're trying to get to New York…" He paused for a beat. "If you want to live, you two should get out of town, also."

Charlotte grimaced at the lady lying on the ground. "Did those wild savages get a hold of her, too?"

Leroy shrugged, and then scratched his head as he gazed over at the car that had slammed into the tree. "I don't know if that man is dead or alive. What's taking the ambulance so doggone long?" He patted his pocket. "Let me borrow your phone; I left mine in the store," he said to Charlotte.

"It's in my handbag—in the car," she said forlornly.

"We don't have phones either," Gabe said. "Lost ours back in Willow Hills while escaping those creatures. You don't get it, do you? The ambulance isn't coming. The EMT workers are either overburdened or they've been bitten themselves. Once those *things* start biting people, it doesn't take long before the infection spreads. From what we've observed, the span between the time they get bitten and the moment they change into a flesh-eater is getting shorter and shorter." Gabe gave a long sigh. "It sounds cold, but we'd all be safer if I put a bullet through her head."

Leroy shot Gabe a murderous look. "That woman can't hurt anybody; she's dead."

"But the dead don't stay dead anymore," Gabe said in a tight, strained voice. "Look, we're headed to New York; you two can stick around here if you want to, or you can come with us. If you have a vehicle in that garage, Leroy, you need to get in it and start heading north."

Mouth turned down, Leroy shook his head. "No thanks. If

people are going crazy, I need to stay right here to guard my property from looters and such."

"Suit yourself," Gabe said. "What about you, Charlotte?"

Charlotte shook her head. "I don't want to go to New York; my family is here in Georgia. Can you folks give me a ride home? I'll pay you for your trouble." Remembering that she didn't have her handbag, she looked down at her empty hands and her face crumpled. "My wallet is in my bag. I don't have any money on me, but I can pay you as soon as we get to my house. Please. It's only twenty miles from here."

From the passenger's seat, Eden gave Charlotte a sympathetic look. "I'm real sorry, Charlotte. We can't take you home, and it's not about money. This town and all the surrounding areas are probably crawling with biters, and once we get on the highway, we can't risk making any detours."

In a fatherly gesture, Leroy patted Charlotte on the back. "Don't worry, little lady. My truck is in the garage, and I'll make sure you get home safely."

"Thanks," Charlotte said, her eyes brimming with tears. "I don't know what I'm gonna tell Chuck's mama? Oh, God, I can still hear his horrible cries. He was yelling and screaming in anguish and there was nothing I could do. I would have helped him if I could, but I barely escaped with my own life. How am I going to tell his mama that a bunch of crazy people mauled him and ate him alive? How can I tell her something as insane as that?"

"I don't know," Leroy whispered hoarsely.

"Leroy, if you're not coming with us, you and Charlotte need to lock yourselves inside the store. It's very likely that the biters are gonna be heading this way, and if you insist on staying, you need to get busy and start boarding up your windows."

Leroy gave Gabe a curious look. "If what you're saying is true…

if dead people are kicking up a ruckus for miles around, then why isn't the government doing something about it? Where's the National Guard?"

"It's happening so fast; I don't think anyone outside this area knows what's going on. All I know is what I've seen with my own eyes. Eden and I both have witnessed how violent and hungry folks become once they've been bitten." He glanced at Charlotte, who was murmuring and wringing her hands in distress. "Now, she knows, too. You heard what she said happened to Chuck."

At the mention of Chuck's name, Charlotte began weeping loudly. Leroy's arm immediately tightened around her; his hand clenching her shoulder comfortingly.

Eden appealed to Leroy's sense of decency. "Leroy, we need to get the baby to a safe place, but we're getting low on gas. We can't fight through that swarm of biters down at the BP station, so can you give us the directions to another nearby gas station?"

"There's a Texaco station on Pelham Avenue." Leroy pointed eastward. "Go a mile or so down the road until you get to Fairfax Street, make a left and then go past two traffic lights. At the second light…" Leroy's voice trailed off as booming sounds exploded from the crashed car that was stalled out on his lawn. The dead man inside was kicking and banging, apparently trying to get out of the car he was trapped inside.

"Oh, my Jesus!" Charlotte screamed.

"What in tarnation?" Eyes bugged out in astonishment, Leroy protectively pulled Charlotte closer.

"Hurry! Get inside the store; they wake up hungry!" Gabe warned Leroy and Charlotte, and then quickly jabbed a button that raised the windows of the Explorer.

"We've got to get to that filling station," Eden said in a panicked voice. She leaned forward and gazed at the gas gauge. "My God, Gabe, the tank is nearly empty."

"I told you we were low."

"You said low…not *empty!*"

"It's not empty. Not quite. We can make it to the Texaco station."

"But suppose we get there and the place is swarming with biters. I don't think we should risk it."

"We can't stick around here," Gabe said emphatically.

Eden watched as Leroy escorted Charlotte across the lawn, grasping her arm as he guided her past the Prius that was rocking back and forth as the irate and famished driver tried to kick and punch his way out of the wreckage.

Eden lowered her window and shouted, "We're coming, Leroy. We're right behind you."

Gabe gave Eden an incredulous look. Eden defiantly stared him down. "I'm not risking my life or Jane's. Together we can help Leroy fortify the windows and doors. Maybe he'll repay us by letting us siphon some gas from his truck."

"Doesn't sound like a good idea."

"Look, you don't get to make all the decisions. I'm not like Charlotte…I'm not some helpless chick that has to depend on a guy to survive. I listen to my instincts," Eden yelled. "I think it's a huge mistake to drive around searching for a filling station in an area that we know is crawling with biters!"

"Okay, you're right; you win," Gabe conceded. "Now calm down, will you?" Gabe put the Explorer in reverse, backed along the pavement, and then swung into the lot.

The baby squirmed in Eden's arms and began screaming at the top of her lungs. Eden gave Jane a bottle and she quieted down, but a sudden explosion of shattering glass caused her to wail again.

Reaching behind his seat, Gabe grabbed the rifle that was hidden beneath a blanket on the floorboard. "He's breaking out of the car! Come on; let's go!"

Eden carried Jane, and the diaper bag was secured over her

shoulder. Gabe held his rifle in one hand, and carried the bags of baby items in the other. Running side by side, Gabe and Eden gasped when a pair of arms groped through the windshield of the banged-up Prius. Next, a blood-covered head emerged.

"Let us in!" Eden yelled, pounding on the red screen door. She looked over her shoulder and yelped when she saw the dead man's shoulders and upper torso determinedly pushing through the opening in the windshield. He hissed and growled, and Eden's first instinct was to reach for her gun. But she couldn't get to it with the baby in her arms. "Shoot him, Gabe!" Eden shouted.

Gabe set the baby supplies on the porch and carefully aimed the rifle. He fired a shot that struck the driver in the skull, taking off the top of his head.

Leroy finally opened the door for Gabe and Eden; he flinched and grimaced when he saw what was left of the driver.

CHAPTER 4

His skin was smooth, the color of burnt sienna with a hint of crimson. With his broad nose, luscious full lips, and strong jawline, Elson Chandler was an undeniably beautiful man. Coils of kinky-curly hair fanned out against the pillow as he slept. Bare-chested and wearing black briefs, Elson was lean and muscular. His athletic body did not require grueling workouts at the gym. Forever young, Elson's good looks had been maintained for over three hundred years.

From the confines of his satin-lined casket, Elson's eyes opened at the sound of footsteps. He smiled faintly. Ismene, his devoted daughter-of-the night, was approaching with a glass of chilled blood. Her typically soft and graceful footsteps were uncharacteristically heavy and fast-paced. He listened intently, scowling as he heard a second set of footfalls that were shuffling and resistant.

"Let me go!" a high-pitched female voice cried.

Bracing himself for trouble, Elson bared his fangs. An instant later, he retracted the strong, sharp teeth and relaxed as he recalled the request he'd made before retiring at dawn: *No refrigerated blood, tonight. I'd like to begin the evening with the taste of warm, living blood, and I expect you to make it happen, Ismene!*

Ismene raised the lid of the solid bronze casket with its gold-plate finish, and Elson was surprised to see four bloody etchings on her slender arm. Gripping the sides of the gleaming coffin, he sat upright, and gazed at her questioningly.

"She scratched me," Ismene responded, nodding at a squirming teenage girl who gawked at Elson through tearful eyes. Streaks of dark mascara and eye shadow smudged her face.

"Why's he lying in a casket?" the girl whined. "What's going on? Are you guys in like...you know...involved in some kind of vampire cult?"

Elson and Ismene shared amused smiles.

"I have to go home; I really have to go," the girl said, and then attempted to wrench herself free. But she couldn't break away from Ismene's vise-like grip. "That cop had no right bringing me to this creepy, old place. If I don't get home soon, my parents are gonna be pissed. My dad's a lawyer, and he'll sue the entire police department for false arrest!"

"A lawyer, huh?" Elson repeated thoughtfully. "Interesting. Perhaps I'll have him draft some contracts for me. I look forward to meeting your father." Elson threw one well-defined thigh and then the other over the side of the coffin and climbed out of his resting place. "How'd we acquire this delectable creature?" he asked Ismene.

"One of the police officers picked her up at the mall; she was apprehended for shoplifting."

"Naughty girl," Elson remarked with amusement.

The girl shook her head adamantly. "I didn't steal anything. I told the cop that there'd been a mistake. I was trying on headbands in Claire's. I paid for all my other stuff...earrings and bracelets, but I forgot about the stupid headband."

"Wrong place; wrong time," Elson commented and then focused on the droplets of blood that trickled down Ismene's arm. "What happened?"

"She attempted to get away, and scratched me," Ismene said with a nonchalant shrug.

"I'll take care of that." Elson reached out. Without question, Ismene extended her arm, and Elson licked away the trails of blood.

The girl cringed. "Oh, gross! Look, there has to be some kind of mistake. I have no idea why that cop brought me here. But my dad's gonna be furious; he's gonna have that idiot's badge, and that's a promise," she yelled bitterly.

Elson looked up, regarding the outraged girl with amusement for a moment, and then returned his attention to Ismene's injured arm. "Your skin is much too beautiful to be scarred." Lowering his head, he swiped his tongue along Ismene's wounds again, licking until the scratch marks miraculously healed.

The girl's eyes widened in shock as she regarded Ismene's suddenly flawless skin. "I wanna go home."

"Relax. You'll be taken home after I've fed," Elson said casually.

"After you've fed! What do you mean? Oh, geez. Don't tell me you guys are like…real vampires. I heard rumors at school, but I didn't believe—"

"Be quiet," Ismene snapped and yanked the girl forward. "Drink, Elson; you need your strength. Tonight is the beginning of your reign and you must be strong and clear-minded."

"No! Wait! Ohmigod, please don't bite me," the girl pleaded, literally jumping up and down with fear. Her voice rose to a frenzied wail. "I wanna go hooome!"

"Shh. Shh. What's your name?" Elson asked quietly.

Refusing to answer, the girl groaned and shook her head.

Elson penetrated her thoughts and discovered her name. "Tessa…pretty name," he said fondly.

"How do you know my name?" she demanded.

"Lucky guess." Gently, he grasped her wrist. "Relax; don't fight it, Tessa. Okay?" His rich, baritone voice was soft and thrillingly seductive.

"No. Don't," Tessa cried. "Let me go. Please. I don't wanna be turned into a vampire."

Elson put a finger under her chin and tilted her head up. "You won't be turned. You have my word." Tessa recoiled from his touch, grimacing as Elson began to run his fingers along the length of her arm. He closed his eyes, enjoying the feeling of the warm blood that pulsed through her veins. Elson's fangs pushed through his gums, and a clicking sound reverberated around the room.

A ragged cry tore from Tessa's throat. "Ohigod, ohmigod! This is insane; this can't be really happening," she babbled in terror.

"Be still and be quiet," Elson commanded, staring hypnotically into his captive's eyes.

Tessa's shoulders slumped in submission. "Okay," she agreed, her brown eyes suddenly vacant.

Elson's gaze wandered down to the pulse at the crook of her elbow. He brought her arm to his mouth and plunged his fangs deeply into her flesh. Under Elson's spell, Tessa's only reaction was a sharp intake of breath.

Ismene observed yearningly as Elson fed on the teenage girl. He drank with great, thirsty gulps, and Ismene involuntarily licked her lips. Sensing her discomfort, Elson withdrew his fangs and said, "Come and join me, my dear."

In an instant, Ismene's slender body was pressed into Tessa's, her fangs deeply embedded in the girl's neck.

⊕ ⊕ ⊕

At seven-fifty in the evening, Bradley M. Jones, Esquire was still at his desk, hunched over a yellow legal pad. Pen in hand, he quibbled over every word of the brief he was preparing. His staff had gone home hours ago, but Bradley had an important case in the morning, and he was willing to work through the night if necessary. He didn't mind working late. In fact, he preferred the solitude of an empty building. His thoughts were clearer in the peaceful environment where there were no ringing phones and no noisy conversations among staff. The ticking of his desk clock and the patter of raindrops that tapped against the window pane were the only audible sounds. There was a certain comfort in being inside, cozy and dry, while the rest of the world dashed around in unpleasant weather.

The annoying buzz of his cell interrupted the quiet. He glanced at the screen and sneered when he saw his estranged wife's name. "What is it, Nicole? Your substantial child support and alimony check isn't due for two weeks."

"Can't you ever be civil?" Nicole complained with a long sigh. "I'm calling about Tessa. She hasn't come home from school."

Bradley's face flushed with sudden anger. "It's eight o'clock in the evening, and you're just noticing that she isn't home?"

"She told me she was going to stop at the mall after school—"

"I'm earning a living—running my firm and actively practicing law, while you lead a life of leisure. Your single obligation is to look after our daughter, but apparently you can't even do that."

"I'm a good mother and you know it!"

Nicole was right; she was a decent enough mother, but Bradley refused to admit it. For all the child support and alimony that came out of his pocket, she should have been a supermom.

"This isn't about us, Bradley. I'm worried sick about Tessa," she said anxiously. "I called all of her friends, but no one has seen or heard from her."

"Maybe she's hanging out with some kids outside her normal circle—you know, the kind of kids that snub their noses at curfew and other rules," Bradley said weakly. His suggestion sounded ludicrous to his own ears. Tessa was a good kid. She was responsible and trustworthy, and she didn't hang out with losers.

"She's had the same group of friends since grade school; she wouldn't suddenly pick up new friends."

"Well, where the heck is she?" he barked, now imagining that his naïve, fifteen-year-old daughter fancied herself in love with some smooth-talking, pimply-faced boy. A boy who was able to persuade her to get in his car and take a ride to Marshall's Peak… or wherever kids went nowadays to make out. Fury washed over him as he imagined his daughter's innocence being stolen in the back seat of a car.

"The mall closed at seven." Nicole's voice cracked. "Do you think we should call the police?"

"Yes, report her missing. I'm leaving the office now; I'll be at the house in fifteen minutes." Bradley disconnected the call.

He snatched his suit jacket off the bronze coat rack and grabbed his umbrella. Dangling his key ring, he hurried out of his office suite and walked swiftly along the corridor. He wanted to be standing in the driveway with the police at his side when the young punk with raging hormones dropped off his daughter. After he finished roughing up the low-life character, he planned to press charges. A night or two in the slammer would give the sleazebag a powerful message: *Bradley M. Jones, Esquire's daughter is strictly off limits.*

Striding urgently toward the stairs, he heard something that sounded like gusts of wind coming from the conference room, and though he was in a rush, the sound emanating from the conference room was too loud and too persistent to ignore. If a member of his staff had carelessly left a window open while sneaking a smoke, there was going to be hell to pay in the morning.

Bradley had built his law firm from the ground up with limited funds and lots of hard work. Allowing a thief easy access to laptops and other expensive office equipment was unconscionable.

Frowning in displeasure, Bradley opened the door. His eyes scanned the darkness and sure enough, one of the windows was open. Blasts of chilly air filled the room. He reached for the light switch, but froze mid-reach and gasped. A form that was blacker than the darkness seemed to be suspended from the ceiling.

"What the—?" In a panic, Bradley flicked on the switch and immediately wished he hadn't. Defying gravity, a black-clad human form was grotesquely clinging to the ceiling like an enormous bat. The tails of its coat whipped and twisted, resembling furled wings. His heart thundering, Bradley gave a cry of shock as he gawked upward.

Aside from its billowing coattails, the coat-clad creature was as immobile as a macabre chandelier. *Sweet Jesus! What is that thing?* Deciding he didn't want to find out, Bradley inched backward, with his umbrella extended for protection. But when the thing ever so slowly turned its head, showing the unnaturally pale face of a man with a leering grin and vicious fangs, Bradley's umbrella clattered to the floor as he made a stumbling run for it.

Racing down the corridor with his heart pounding out of his chest, Bradley heard a heavy thud behind him. The monstrous being had dropped to the floor. The high ceiling in the conference room made for a pretty long fall, and he prayed that the beastly intruder had been critically injured. Or killed! But all hope was instantly dashed when something grabbed him by the shoulder. He was suddenly lifted from the floor by strong hands with nails like curved daggers. The nails sank into his flesh...down to the bone. Overtaken by blinding agony, Bradley shrieked in pain and terror.

CHAPTER 5

The darkening sky loomed ominously. Nerves rattled from the horrors he'd witnessed in the past few hours, Leroy kept peering through the windows, hoping to see a police car, but help had yet to arrive.

Turning away from the window, Leroy asked Gabe, "Are you sure that fella was all the way dead before you shot his head off? It's possible he was merely trying to free himself from the car he was trapped inside."

Gabe gave a frustrated sigh. "He came back from the dead, and if I hadn't shot him, he'd be having us for dinner."

Leroy called 9-1-1 for the umpteenth time. "Line's still busy! What kind of crap is that?"

Charlotte glanced at Leroy. "Can I borrow your phone, again— I don't know why I'm having such a hard time getting through to my parents."

Leroy handed Charlotte his phone. "Here you go. Keep trying until you get through; I can use the landline phone to try and get a hold of the police." He marched over to a wall-mounted, old-fashioned pay phone that Eden had assumed was part of the décor and only for show. He plunked change into the coin slot and turned the rotary dial with his finger.

"My calls keep going to voicemail," Charlotte complained, shaking her head. "I'm afraid to call Chuck's mama…I'm not ready to talk to her yet." Wringing her hands fretfully, she wandered toward the window and stared out as if entranced.

"I'll be danged! I finally got through to 9-1-1, but instead of talking to a live person, they got me listening to a recorded message," Leroy groused, standing in front of the pay phone.

Noticing that Jane had fallen asleep, Eden tucked her inside an empty cardboard box. "While we're waiting to get through to the police, we should start boarding up the windows," Eden suggested after sheltering Jane in the baby products aisle. "Do you have any lumber around here, Leroy?" she asked, glancing around.

Frustrated, Leroy hung up the phone with a bang. "Can't get a dang human being on the phone; I hate talking to machines."

"We need lumber…for the windows," Eden repeated. "Do you have any?"

Leroy nodded. "I've got some lumber in the garage. It's only flimsy plywood, though…nothing sturdy."

"That'll work; it's better than nothing," Gabe said. "Let's take a look around the garage."

"Ohmigod!" Charlotte screamed, backing away from the window. "Th— That dead lady. Sh—she's moving."

Leroy, Eden, and Gabe all raced to the window. Gazing over the top of the big, neon clock, they gawked in shock as the bloodied woman propped herself up and slowly clambered to her feet. Gabe groaned in distress. "I should have put a bullet through her head while she was down."

The dead woman in the blood-stained dress stood motionless for a few seconds, and then looked around confusedly. As if unsure of what to do or where to go, she took slow, unsteady steps, jerkily making her way toward the pavement. She stopped and regarded the Explorer in the parking lot, teetering slightly as she snatched at the empty air, as if trying to catch hold of something—anything—edible. A flock of birds flew overhead, and she emitted snarls and coarse hisses as she futilely groped toward the sky.

"Lord, almighty!" Leroy exclaimed. "What would cause a dead woman to get up and start walking around?" His questioning gaze moved from Eden to Gabe.

"Shh! Keep your voice down!" Gabe urged in a stern whisper. "Maybe she'll wander away, and spare us from having to waste any bullets."

Charlotte let out a frightened shriek and uttered, "Oh, no!" Astonishingly, a pack of men and woman wearing clothes that were ripped and blood-spattered were lumbering down the street. What distinguished them from the living was the awkward way they walked, the grayish hue of their skin, and the horrific growls and other inarticulate sounds they emitted.

Unlike the woman in pink, this herd of flesh-eaters didn't appear to be indecisive or faltering as they moved in tandem toward the grocery store.

"Get away from the window. They know we're in here," Gabe shouted.

In his haste to duck down quickly, Leroy knocked the neon clock out of the window, and when it crashed to the floor, Jane let out a strident wail. Alerted by the baby's cries, the gruesome herd hastened their ungainly movements.

"Charlotte, I need you to look after Jane. Feed her and check her diaper…can you do that for me?" Eden asked as she groped through the diaper bag and then pulled out her gun.

"Uh-huh," Charlotte replied weakly.

Eden tossed Charlotte the diaper bag. Looking over her shoulder, Charlotte scurried to the baby products aisle where Jane screamed nonstop.

Sitting in a heap on the floor and wearing a stricken expression, Leroy shook his head and mumbled. "I can't believe this is happening. It's like it's the end of the world out there; I've never seen anything like this."

"Get a grip, Leroy," Gabe barked. "Where are your weapons? I know you keep some kind of protection around here."

"Yeah, I have a gun," he muttered, while looking dazed.

"Well, go get it, man. We have to take those creatures out before they break into the store."

The notion of the undead breaking in and vandalizing his store seemed to bring Leroy out of his stupor. Enlivened, he jumped to his feet and rushed behind the counter. He emerged holding a shiny automatic, and there was a newfound look of determination in his eyes.

Gabe, Eden, and Leroy ran out of the store and lined up on the porch. Gabe took the first shot; his bullet struck one of the undead that was dressed in the bright orange uniform of a roadway construction worker. The construction worker had on a neon-yellow hard hat and was carrying a stack of traffic cones. Hit between the eyes, the construction worker went down like a sack of potatoes; the yellow hat tumbled off his head, and the traffic cones fell from his arms and rolled around the ground.

"Bull's eye!" Gabe chortled. "You gotta aim for the head, Leroy," Gabe explained.

Eden fired off two rounds that struck a biter in the neck and arm. Taking a risk, she ran off the porch to get a better shot.

"Eden, no!" Gabe shouted, but she ignored him. Holding her gun with her arms outstretched, she moved closer to her target. The next bullet she fired hit him in the side of the head, exploding his brain.

"We have to back her up," Gabe yelled to Leroy. Leroy hesitantly left the safety of the porch and followed Gabe out onto the lawn.

More agile and swift than the creatures that threatened her, Eden ran around the yard, firing shots at close range. After emptying her gun, she stepped back and let Gabe and Leroy finish off the herd of flesh-eaters. Leroy took the final shot. Ironically, it was the lady in pink, the woman whose life he'd struggled to save a short while ago.

Eden nodded with satisfaction as she observed the unmoving bodies that now littered the sidewalk, parking lot, and the lawn.

"You guys go in the garage and see about that lumber. Also, grab anything we can use as weapons: shovels, hammers, axes… After I check on Jane and Charlotte, I'll help you board up the windows." She turned to go inside and then turned back around. "How come you don't have bars up at the windows or one of those steel gates in front of the door?" Eden asked Leroy.

"I have an alarm system, and I have grates across the windows in the back of the store, but having steel bars and such in the front would ruin the aesthetics of Leroy's Place. Doesn't fit in with the quaint and homey look."

Shaking her head, Eden pulled open the screen door.

"I'm starting to wonder who wears the pants in your relationship," Leroy said snidely to Gabe.

"We're not in a relationship," Gabe answered. "We're just two people who met up while trying to survive this madness."

"You may let her walk all over you, but I'm not accustomed to taking orders from a teenage girl."

"Eden knows what she's doing, and I advise you to listen to her…that is, if you want to stay alive."

CHAPTER 6

ith no recollection of physically leaving his office, Bradley found himself slumped in a chair inside a strange room. *Where am I?* Weak and disoriented, he looked around the unfamiliar surroundings. An array of candles illuminated the room, and the furnishings were old-fashioned. It had a fifties...perhaps a sixties vibe, and judging by the musty odor, the room hadn't been occupied in decades. *What is this place...an old hotel?* Through squinted eyes, he surveyed his environment. There were two neatly-made twin beds, a sturdy wood desk, an unlit lamp with a pleated shade, and yellowing wallpaper with water stains. The sign on the door read: *Welcome to The Lilac. Check-Out Time is 12 Noon.*

As suspected, this was indeed a hotel room, albeit a decrepit and outdated one. Wait a minute! The Lilac was an old, rundown building downtown; it had been abandoned for years. What the heck was he doing in a vacant hotel? He shook his head, trying to get his bearings.

Tessa's missing! That sudden flash of memory prompted him to his feet. A fragment of another memory caused Bradley to shudder. Searching his mind, he recalled being attacked by something ghoulish and inhuman inside his law firm.

Hit by a desperate urge to escape, he jerked forward, his body poised to run. But a shock of pain radiating from his shoulders halted his movement, causing his knees to sag.

He gingerly touched the source of the pain and flinched. A warm, sticky fluid oozed through ragged holes that penetrated the luxurious fabric of his tailor-made jacket. He gazed at his blood-covered palm, wondering if he'd been stabbed in each shoulder. Desperate to get out of the dreary hotel, Bradley staggered to the door and twisted the knob. Shockingly, the door was locked. In a panic, he turned the knob back and forth. "Let me out of here," he shouted.

At the sound of approaching footsteps, he let go of the knob. He raised his hands defensively when a key turned the lock.

Bradley backed up as the door opened slowly. He stood flabbergasted as three grim-faced teens—a lean bodied male and two eerily beautiful females—glided across the threshold.

"What's the matter with you kids…are you on drugs or something? If this is a prank, it's not very funny. Kidnapping is a serious crime, and you could all end up behind bars for a long time!"

"This is no prank, Mr. Jones. We're dead serious," said the male, who seemed to be the leader of the trio. The young man's eyes were dark and filled with menace. The eyes of his two female cohorts were also hardened and unforgiving.

Bradley rubbed his injured, right shoulder and then the left, as his mind searched for a solution—a way to reason with these diabolical kids. One of the girls…a pale beauty with deadly blue eyes swiped her finger across the wound on Bradley's left shoulder. Appallingly, she licked the blood from her finger and then gave him a taunting smile.

He was reminded of Charles Manson and his diabolical female accomplices and was instantly filled with dread. What would these crazy kids do next—use his blood to write profanities on the wall?

"Tessa's here," the male leader said in a detached manner.

"My daughter's here?" Bradley asked, his voice filled with a mixture of surprise and horror.

"Yeah, she's hanging out with us," responded the pale girl.

"What have you done to her?"

"Nothing much; she's cool."

"What do you mean, she's cool. If you've hurt my daughter—"

"Chill out, man. Your daughter's fine. By the way, my name's Elson...Elson Chandler." Elson extended his hand. Bradley refused the gesture, crossing his arms in front of him, and protectively cupping the deep and painful gauges in both his shoulders.

Elson withdrew his hand and shrugged. "This is Ismene and her sister, Lisette," he said wearing a gracious smile.

Bradley gave the so-called sisters a curious look. One was African-American and the other, with her light hair and glacial blue eyes, was a willowy girl, and pale as a Swede. *Sisters, my eye...more like sisters in crime*, he thought sardonically. "Listen, I've been wounded by...by a creature of some sort, and I need medical attention."

"Not a problem," Elson replied.

"And I want to see my daughter; I need to know she's all right."

"Requesting medical attention is one thing, but demanding we release the hostage is asking a lot, Mr. Attorney At Law," Ismene said mockingly.

Bradley winced at the word *hostage*. "Why do you want to keep Tessa?" His face crinkled in confusion.

"She's collateral." Elson gave a slight smile; his eyes, however, were cold. "What can you offer in exchange for your daughter?"

"Are you asking me to pay ransom to get Tessa back?"

"Not exactly; you see, it's not your money I'm after."

"Then, what do you want?"

"I want to obtain your legal services. There's some property I'm interested in—"

"This is an outrage," Bradley interrupted. He'd lost his patience with these kooks. "Are you kids out of your minds? You abducted my daughter in hopes that I would oversee a real estate transaction? I should have you all arrested. Do you realize that I'm the top criminal defense attorney in this area?" Puffed up with self-importance, Bradley scanned the faces of his captors. They didn't look impressed, and judging from their hardened expressions, they were deeply offended. A cold sweat broke out on his face. He should have chosen his words more carefully. Stammering, he softened his approach. "You kids…should…you know… Well, you're too young to be concerned with adult matters. You're only young for a short while. You should be going to parties and leading carefree lives," he said with a forced smile.

Elson scowled. "Looks can be deceiving. We're a lot older than we look."

"As I said, real estate law isn't my forte, but I'd be happy to recommend someone with real estate expertise. Now, please…be reasonable. Let me take my daughter home."

Elson shook his head gravely. "Tessa's not going anywhere, Mr. Jones. Not until you and I come to a conclusion. And by the way, you should reserve your histrionics for the courtroom. That temper tantrum you displayed a few minutes ago was unbecoming and unprofessional. Don't let it happen again."

Bradley wiped perspiration from his forehead. This young punk named Elson Chandler was delusional. He was certain that Elson and the two girls were on some kind of drugs. Drugs or not, one thing was for certain—they were demented and dangerous and had to be handled with kid gloves. "I apologize. I lost my head," he conceded. "It's just that…well, I'm worried sick about Tessa."

"As you should be," Elson said ominously. "But hysterics won't help you or your daughter." He clapped his hands together and shouted, "Chaos!"

Seconds later, a pallid-faced brute with a mass of kinky hair and a familiar, leering grin burst through the door.

"Greetings, Chaos," Elson said.

"What's up, man?" Chaos replied quickly, and then took a few running steps and seemed to glide in midair toward Bradley. His hands, with long and deadly claws, rested at his sides. He was wearing black jeans, black boots, a black shirt, and oddly...a black tuxedo jacket with tails that flapped like wings. His sharp and lethal fangs glistened with saliva, and his eyes burned with hunger.

Chaos, it turned out, was the same vile creature that had come through the window of the conference room and had managed to hang bizarrely from the ceiling. The psycho landed heavily in front of Bradley. Mindful of the pain that Chaos could inflict, Bradley cowered and shielded his face. "Get this maniac away from me. I'll look at the contracts; I'll do anything you want!"

Elson chuckled. "Wise choice, Mr. Jones. Oh, and by the way, Chaos is not a maniac; he's a vampire, just like the rest of us." He gestured toward Ismene and Lisette. "If he seems a bit ferocious, it's only because he hasn't fed this evening."

These kids are certifiable lunatics! They actually believe they're vampires. Bradley stole a glance at Chaos and shuddered. The kid was enormous; he was well over six feet with lots of bulk, and he was strong as an ox. Chaos gazed at Bradley through eyes as dark as his corrupt soul. Scaling walls and hanging from ceilings were circus tricks, and Bradley figured that the hulky teen was on steroids or something.

Tauntingly, Chaos licked his lips, and Bradley grimaced at the sight of his slimy, gray tongue. A cold chill went through him as he imagined this band of deviants taunting and terrorizing his daughter. "Can I see Tessa?" he asked in a voice choked with emotion. Tessa was probably out of her mind with fear. She'd led a pretty sheltered and cushy life, and to his knowledge, the worst she'd ever experience was the death of her kitten, Muffy…and of course, his and her mother's divorce.

"Your daughter's resting right now. You know, recharging and regaining her strength," Ismene responded with a smirk.

A look of horror crossed Bradley's face. "Why does she need to regain her strength? What's happened to her?" His mouth stretched open, and he began to yell, "TESSA! TESSA! Don't worry, honey, Dad's here. I'm taking you home, sweetheart. Everything's going to be all right." His words of bravado rang false because there was nothing Bradley could do. Feeling helpless, he dropped his head into his hands briefly, and then looked up. "I'm ready to cooperate. Give me the paperwork for the real estate deal. I'll look over it."

"Not so fast, Counselor," Lisette interjected. "Elson's real estate interests are huge. Handling his affairs requires legal expertise and ruthless cunning. Are you the man for the job?"

"I am."

"Pro bono, of course."

"Of course," Bradley murmured dully.

Elson began to pace back and forth. In deep thought, he cradled his chin. After a few minutes, he stood still and cast his gaze on Bradley. "Consider yourself very lucky. I could have transfixed you with my eyes and willed you to do my bidding, but I want you to be in possession of a sound mind when you transfer the deed to the Sherman Mansion into my name."

Bradley looked dumbstruck. "You can't be serious."

Elson rubbed his hands together gleefully. "I'm quite serious. That fine example of Georgian architecture suits my needs perfectly. As soon as the paperwork is complete, I want the Sherman name removed from the gilded gate and replaced with the Chandler insignia."

"The Sherman Mansion is a historical landmark, owned by the city of Frombleton. It's open to the public for tours and exhibits, and the city earns a large portion of its revenue when the mansion is rented for weddings, receptions, luncheons, and meetings. With all due respect, sir...the Sherman Mansion isn't for sale; your request is ludicrous!"

Taken aback, Elson winced. He glanced at Ismene. "What did that fool say?"

"In so many words, the counselor called you crazy," Ismene replied, shooting Bradley a look of contempt.

Bradley began to backpedal quickly. "No, no, I didn't mean it that way. I'm not saying you're crazy. But the idea...what you're proposing is preposterous."

Elson smiled indulgently. "I'm a visionary, Mr. Jones. Nothing I contemplate is preposterous. I heard you were considered a barracuda in the courtroom, but apparently that was merely a rumor." Elson's smile quickly faded. He directed his attention to Chaos. "My throat is parched, and I know you're thirsty, too. Go get the girl."

With supernatural swiftness, Chaos exited the room. A few minutes later, he returned, carrying a moaning, semiconscious Tessa. He dumped her on one of the beds, where she lay looking crumpled and lifeless.

"Tessa!" Bradley rushed to his daughter's side. Leaning over her, he gaped in disbelief. Blood splotches stained her clothing, her face was a sickly, purplish color, and her eyes were sunken with dark circles. When Bradley noticed the puncture marks that marred her neck and arms, he gasped in horror. "What did you monsters do to her?" Gripping her shoulder, he frantically shook Tessa. "Wake up, Tessa! Sweetheart, please wake up."

Tessa gave a long, agonized whine. Her eyelids fluttered briefly, but didn't open. Bradley glared at Elson. "This sick joke has gone too far. I demand that my daughter be taken to the hospital." He stuck a hand in the pocket of his jacket, withdrew his cell phone, and hastily tapped the screen.

"Who do you think you're calling?" Ismene became a blur of motion as she whizzed across the room and snatched the phone from Bradley's hand. She peered at the screen and then looked at Elson. "He was trying to call the police."

"Is that so?" Holding Bradley in his heated gazed, Elson sauntered over to the twin bed.

"I wasn't calling the police; I was trying to get an ambulance for my daughter. Look at her! She's barely breathing; she needs medical attention."

"You'd like to see me handcuffed and arrested, wouldn't you, Mr. Jones?" Elson said in a soft hiss of a voice. "You want me to spend a night or two in the slammer, don't you?"

"I didn't say that."

"We vampires are more than eternally beautiful creatures. We possess many gifts…like mindreading. Chaos listened to your thoughts earlier tonight…after you spoke to Nicole."

Bradley winced in surprise, and then collected himself. *Merely an educated guess. These obnoxious hooligans can't read minds. Any fool could have guessed that Nicole and I would converse after our daughter had gone missing.*

"We *hooligans*, as you refer to us, can absolutely probe the human mind. We don't have to rely on 'educated guesses,' as you presumed," Elson scoffed.

Christ! Is this nutcase actually reading my mind?

"Yes, I am. We all are," Elson responded to Bradley's inner musing. The two sisters crept up slowly, almost seductively as they once again flanked Elson. The grinning fiend called Chaos closed the door and locked it, and then began striding forward with lofty arrogance.

Panicked, Bradley thought about charging for the door, yanking the chain away, and running like hell toward the main entrance… wherever that was. But he couldn't leave Tessa behind.

A cold sweat ran down his face in rivulets. Helplessly, he staggered backward, using the sleeve of his jacket to mop away the perspiration. Bradley gulped fearfully as the ghoulish teens closed in on him. Still smiling, Chaos licked his lips with a darkened tongue. There was a ravenous, inhuman look in his eyes. As absurd as it seemed, Bradley began to accept that these kids weren't merely wayward, mean-spirited teens. *They really are vampires!* A hoarse sob escaped his throat when the sisters leapt forward. Attacking him, they inexplicably pulled his jacket off, and then tossed it on the bed next to Tessa, who uttered soft, incoherent sounds as she drifted in and out of a troubled sleep.

In a frenzy of madness, the sisters used razor-sharp fingernails to shred and rip the shirt from Bradley's back. Now bare from the waist up, he held out his hands defensively, his heart kicking violently inside his chest as he backed away. The girls advanced, and he could see his fearful expression reflected in their cruel eyes.

"The counselor requested medical treatment," Elson said in a humorous tone. "Fulfill his request, girls."

"We'll heal you," Lisette whispered, grasping Bradley's arm. He shivered as her icy fingers traveled upward to one of his injured shoulders. She caressed the bloody gouges, and then lowered her head and pressed her chilled lips against the wounds and began to suck. Pain radiated through his body and Bradley let out a shriek. The shriek quieted down to choking gasps when Chaos, bearing fangs that dripped with saliva, lunged for him. Bradley passed out when he felt Chaos's sharp teeth tearing into his neck.

CHAPTER 7

The sky had grown gloomy, as if it might rain. Eden couldn't imagine how they'd deal with biters in bad weather. She rushed to the baby products aisle and was relieved to find Charlotte sitting on the floor, holding Jane close.

Charlotte pulled herself to her feet when she heard Eden approaching. "Those gunshots were driving me nuts; I was scared out of my wits, but thank God, you're okay. What happened to Leroy and your boyfriend? Please tell me they're all right."

"Gabe's not my boyfriend; we're just friends," Eden said. "But, yeah…he and Leroy are fine. They're getting some stuff that we need out of the garage." Eden took Jane from Charlotte and kissed the fussy infant. "It's going to be all right, Jane," she cooed. "I'm not going to let anything happen to you."

"Did you guys, uh, did you kill all those *things?*" Charlotte asked with her face scrunched in disgust.

"Yeah, we got 'em, but who knows how many more are out there."

"You'd think with all that gunfire, someone would have called the police." Charlotte held up Leroy's cell phone. "I've tried and tried, but I can't get through to anyone. I've tried calling everyone I can think of—my parents, friends, even Chuck's mama, but all I get is their voicemail."

Charlotte stood up. "Look, instead of boarding up windows,

we should be trying to escape. Seriously...being holed up in this store is driving me crazy."

"This is the safest place to be right now. We can't risk driving around, looking for gas when we don't know how many biters are out there."

"Where did those biter-things come from?" Charlotte asked.

"I don't know, but they're spreading fast."

Charlotte's eyes filled with tears. "It's my fault."

"Why do you say that?"

"Because Chuck didn't want to come here today...he had a meeting with an important client, and he wanted to eat near his office, but I coaxed him into coming. It's like I always have to push him to his limit, just to see how much he cares." She dropped her eyes and twisted her engagement ring fretfully. "And now he's gone. Just like that...he's gone." She snapped her fingers. "I have to cancel my wedding and my mama is going to flip! Invitations have already been sent, dresses ordered, and the venue was rented a year ago. Everything's in place, but I don't have my groom anymore." Charlotte began to sob. "Mama and Daddy have spent a fortune on my big day, and they're going to be sick when I tell them the wedding is off."

Eden patted Charlotte on the back, unsure if she were consoling her over the tragic loss of her fiancé or for her soon-to-be cancelled wedding. "Charlotte, you're not going to get a chance to talk to your folks at all if you don't put all your energy into staying alive."

The front door opened, and there was banging and thumping as Gabe and Leroy unloaded the plywood and tools they'd found in the garage. Eden returned Jane to her makeshift, cardboard bassinette. "Come on, Charlotte. We have to help board up those windows." She looked down at Charlotte's bare feet. "Maybe

Leroy has a pair of women's shoes in the garage or somewhere."

Standing at the front of the store, Gabe held up a nail gun and smiled at Eden. "This is for you—to conserve your strength, princess warrior," Gabe said with laughter. "Leroy and I will take care of hammering nails the old-fashioned way."

Being called Princess Warrior was a compliment, but Eden could feel her face reddening with embarrassment. Taking the spotlight off herself, she asked Leroy if he happened to have any women's shoes. "For Charlotte," she added.

Leroy's glanced down at Charlotte's bare feet. "Hmm." He pondered for a few seconds and then said, "I do have something in the storage room." He strode to the back of the store and disappeared behind a set of doors. He emerged carrying a box. "I've got about fifty pairs of flip flops in here, all inscribed with "Leroy's Place." At $15.99 a pop, they didn't go over too well with my clientele, so I dropped the price to five dollars—but still no luck. Folks preferred my sandwiches to my footwear, and so I started giving them away with every purchase. I can't believe I still have a box full of those dang flip flops." He motioned for Charlotte. "Come on and help yourself, little lady. Look through the pile; I'm sure you'll find your size and your favorite color." Leroy was trying to lift Charlotte's spirits, which was commendable under the circumstances.

Charlotte looked horrified and then resigned to replacing her expensive designer heels with a pair of cheap flip flops.

"Did you ask him about loaning us some gasoline," Eden whispered to Gabe.

"I asked, but he wouldn't go for it. He says he only has a half-tank of gas in his pickup truck, and that he has to get Charlotte home to her family if a rescue team doesn't come through."

"No rescue team is coming for us. And driving Charlotte home may be a wasted trip. I mean, think about it, Charlotte can't get in touch with anyone, and I wouldn't be surprised if the biters have already gotten to her family."

"We don't know that," Gabe said optimistically. "Maybe we should pool our resources...you know, maybe we should all travel to her parents' home together. While we're there, we can notify the authorities about the plague of biters in the Willow Hills area. After that...you and I and Jane will head for New York."

Eden nodded. "Sounds good, but we can't all fit in a pickup truck. We'll have to take the Explorer, and that brings us back to square one...we still need Leroy to share his gas with us."

"I'll run it by him after we board up the windows."

"Okay, good." Eden picked up a few pieces of wood and the nail gun, and began working on one of the smaller windows while Gabe and Leroy boarded up the large, picture window.

"The door behind the screen door looks like wood, but it's made of solid steel," Leroy said proudly. "But we're gonna have to find something to cover the windows in the back. My living quarters upstairs should be all right. Those creatures can't climb, can they?" Leroy asked worriedly.

"Can they climb?" Charlotte echoed, her anxious eyes locked on Gabe.

"Haven't seen them climbing anything. I don't think they're capable," Gabe said reassuringly. "From what I've experienced, it seems they can hear and possibly smell, but they only see what's in their direct line of vision."

"This is dreadful; I can't wait to get home," Charlotte murmured and passed Leroy a nail. Wearing bright blue flip flops, Charlotte's idea of pitching in was to hand Leroy nails. Jane announced that she was awake with a strong, healthy yell, and Charlotte promptly set down the box of nails and went to attend to her.

Gabe chose that opportunity to tell Leroy about his and Eden's idea to pool their resources.

"But you still want to siphon my gas!" Leroy said with a scowl. "I can't go along with that. How am I supposed to get around?"

"You're coming with us, aren't you?" Eden inquired.

"There's no point in all of us escorting Charlotte home. I only offered because you two turned her down."

Gabe groaned in frustration. "Leroy, be reasonable, man. We don't know how many biters are out there, and Eden is out of ammo. I only have one box of bullets for my rifle, and they won't last forever...and eventually, your ammo is gonna run out, too. What I'm trying to say is, we can't stay here forever. Eventually, we're going to have to move on, and it's much safer to travel in a group."

"I'm not traveling, period! Leroy's Place is my livelihood—a good business that was passed down to me by my daddy, Leroy Hawthorne, Sr. The land this place is on has been in my family for generations, and I'm not letting a bunch of growling savages run me off my property!"

Leroy slammed down his hammer and stomped away. "Any luck with the cell phone?" he asked Charlotte who was sitting in a chair behind the counter, rocking Jane.

"The signal is going in and out, and even when I get one, I can't get through to anyone. I tried the pay phone, but it doesn't have a dial tone anymore."

"Dang! I'm going upstairs to see if the local news is covering this crisis. Maybe there's a broadcast telling folks what to do." Leroy left the main room. His weary footsteps could be heard as he slowly trudged up the stairs.

"I'm going out back to check the grates on the windows—make sure they're sturdy," Gabe told Eden.

Eden nodded and began piling the leftover wood in a corner.

Next, she propped a shovel, an ax, a three-foot pipe iron, various-sized hammers, and a nail gun against the wall near the front door. Before joining Charlotte and Jane behind the counter, she gave the assemblage of weapons a last glance, and decided that the nail gun and the ax would be her weapons of choice if the biters tried to attack.

Jane gurgled contentedly and Eden took her from Charlotte's arms. "How's my girl? How's my baby?" she said, nuzzling Jane. "You smell so good," she commented, and then covered the baby's face with kisses.

"She's nice and dry and her tummy's full," Charlotte commented with a smile as she observed Eden lovingly interacting with the baby. "I've been meaning to ask you something?"

"What's on your mind?"

"Where's Jane's mother?"

Eden lowered her head. "She died," she murmured uncomfortably.

"How?"

"Domestic abuse," Eden said, deciding that Charlotte was too frazzled to handle the truth about Jane's mother. In her current state of mind, Eden was pretty sure Charlotte would freak out if she knew that Jane's mother had turned into a biter.

"Was she murdered by her husband?"

Eden nodded.

"Did he beat her to death or did he shoot her?" Frowning, Charlotte shook her head briskly. "Never mind; I don't want to know. Anyway, how did you end up with Jane? Are you a relative?"

"Uh-huh, we're cousins."

"How old are you?" Charlotte narrowed her eyes slightly. "You look barely out of high school."

"I'm almost eighteen."

"That's so young to have the responsibility of an infant."

"I'm doing the best I can."

"You're doing great, but seventeen is awfully young to be saddled down with a kid."

"Almost eighteen," Eden reminded. She didn't know what Charlotte was getting at, but she felt the urge to hold Jane to her chest and hug her possessively. She was growing attached to Jane, and the idea of handing her over to an adoption agency in New York no longer seemed like a good idea.

CHAPTER 8

The bedraggled man and woman Jonas had rescued from the cornfields were incapable of verbal communication. They had lost all of the traits that made them human, and could only make a series of grunting sounds that indicated ravenous hunger. Having the instincts of wild animals, they became crazed by the scent of blood.

Keeping them away from people, Jonas guided them to the woods and allowed them to feed on small creatures until nightfall. And then, under the shroud of darkness, he led the awkwardly-moving pair to the isolated, old sugar mill that he and Zac had briefly used as a hiding place. While they munched on rabbit and squirrel, Jonas locked the unsightly pair inside, and then walked back to his hotel.

⊕ ⊕ ⊕

Holland threw on a denim jacket and popped her head in the kitchen. "I'm going out, Mom."

With a worried expression, Phoebe looked up from her laptop. "The sun has gone down; it's too late to go out."

"Vamps can't hurt me; you know that."

"But what about the force field—how are you going to get through that?"

"Easily. I'm a witch, remember? I'm gonna walk right through it. I'm bouncing off the walls, Mom. I need to get some fresh air and clear my head."

Phoebe gave her daughter a sympathetic look. "I guess you still haven't heard from Jonas."

"Not a word," Holland said glumly. "But don't worry about me; I'll be all right."

Phoebe rose and placed an arm around Holland's shoulder. "I'm your mother; I can't help from worrying about you." She walked with Holland to the living room and grasped her hand. "Hon, I don't know what's going on with Jonas, but I don't like seeing you like this."

"I said I'm okay," Holland whined in annoyance.

"No, you're not. And if it'll make you feel a little better, I want you to know that when Jonas set off on that impossible mission to get you out of Stoneham, I warned him about the power those witches possessed. Know what he said?"

Holland lifted a brow.

"He said…and I quote him: 'Nothing is stronger than the power of love.' I thought you needed to hear that."

"Thanks, Mom," Holland replied quietly. His confession of love was nice to hear, but didn't change the fact that Holland was sad and lonely. She solemnly opened the door and easily walked through the force field. Looking back at her mother, she gave her a wave and a sad smile.

Unable to penetrate the protective field that Holland's mentor had put around their home as a vampire deterrent, Phoebe stood in the doorway and blew her daughter a kiss. "Please be careful, hon."

"I will," Holland said, and trotted down the steps. Walking briskly in the early evening moonlight, her cell phone pinged. Hoping for a message from Jonas, she stared at the screen anxiously.

She was instantly disappointed when she noticed that the text was from her classmate, Doreen.

I have juicy gossip. Meet me at my locker in the morning.

Holland wasn't the least bit interested in gossip—not at the moment. All she wanted was to hear Jonas's voice. Was that asking for too much?

She had hoped that getting out of the house and feeling the crisp night air would lift her spirits, but gloom and loneliness continued to engulf her. Times like this, she would have headed straight down the path that led to Naomi's house. But Naomi was gone forever, and Holland doubted she'd ever stop mourning the loss of her best friend.

Thinking about the way that conniving vampire family, the Sullivans, had preyed on Naomi and her parents filled Holland with rage. The Sullivans had befriended Naomi and her parents, inviting them to exclusive social gatherings, knowing all along that their true intentions were to turn Naomi into one of the living dead. They wanted Naomi as an eternal mate for their vampire son.

Infuriated, and wanting to take her anger out on a bloodsucker, Holland walked boldly in the night. *Any stupid vampire that has the gall to sink its fangs into me will be in for a painful surprise.* She was so irate, she was certain she could take on an entire gang of vampires, if she had to.

As she neared the end of her block, she saw a familiar person walking swiftly toward her, and when she realized it was her chatterbox neighbor, Mrs. Murphy, Holland thought about walking in the opposite direction. But before she could turn around, she and Mrs. Murphy were face to face.

Braced for a long-winded conversation, Holland sighed and greeted her neighbor. "How are you, Mrs. Murphy?"

Surprisingly, Mrs. Murphy muttered, "Just fine," and kept moving without breaking her stride.

Holland turned around and watched as Mrs. Murphy crossed the street and speed-walked along Abercorn Road. Apparently, Mrs. Murphy was getting in her evening exercise.

Holland turned right onto Mill Stream Court and noticed newlyweds, Amy and Derek Horsheck, as they came out of their house, rushing toward their driveway. Holland waved, but the couple seemed to be in too much of a hurry to return the greeting. Derek opened the car door and then gestured impatiently. "Get a move on, Amy; we're gonna be late."

"I'm coming; I'm coming," Amy said as she rushed to the passenger's side of the car.

"Hi, Amy," Holland greeted with another hand wave.

Startled, Amy jerked around. "Oh, hi, Holland; you scared the living daylights out of me," Amy said with a nervous chuckle.

"Get in the damn car!" Derek bellowed.

"Gotta go; good to see you, Holland." There was a forced smile on Amy's face as she gazed at Holland through haunted eyes.

Okay, what's going on? Why is everyone in a rush? Curiosity getting the best of her, Holland shamelessly stared as Derek and Amy yanked their seatbelts across their bodies. Looking panicked, Derek looked over his shoulder and backed out of the driveway. The tires squealed as the car peeled off.

In the distance, she noticed indistinct shapes and figures flitting about in the shadows. There were more people than usual out tonight. No one seemed to be moving at a leisurely pace. Everyone seemed to be racing to get somewhere. But where? Had people finally come to realize that there were dangerous vampires living among them? And were they all trying to get safely inside before the vampires came out? But Amy and Derek were leaving their house, so that theory didn't make sense.

Curious to know if Doreen's juicy gossip had anything to do with the odd behavior she was seeing tonight, Holland pulled her cell from her jacket pocket and pressed Doreen's number. "Hey, Doreen," Holland said when Doreen picked up. "I was wondering if your news has anything to do with, uh, the vamps."

"We can't discuss vampires on the phone…especially not at night! Geez, Holland, use common sense. I'll talk to you in the morning…when the sun is shining," Doreen said gruffly.

"It's just that I'm noticing more people than usual out tonight, and you should see the way they're all rushing around. It's weird. They're acting like New Yorkers or people from some other fast-paced city. I can't help thinking—" Holland's voice was drowned out by blaring car horns. At the traffic light, an impatient driver cut in front of the cars that were at a standstill, and roared away, leaving behind a trail of disgruntled motorists.

"Are you outside, Holland?" Doreen asked.

"Yeah, people are acting really weird out here tonight. Cars are whizzing past and pedestrians are zooming like they're trying to get to the finish line in a 10K race."

"I told you, you should stay inside at night."

"I know, but I got restless."

"Obviously, you didn't take the information I shared with you very seriously."

"Yes, I do. But—"

"For your own sake, Holland, get off the streets, and go home!"

The phone went dead and Holland didn't know if the call dropped or if Doreen had angrily hung up on her. She noticed that people were still moving about with a sense of urgency, as if all of them were being drawn in the same direction by a sinister, magnetic pull. The vibe in the air was growing creepier by the second, and going home was starting to seem like a good idea.

The moment she returned the phone to her pocket, it buzzed in her hand.

Assuming Doreen was calling again, Holland held the phone to her ear and said, "Sorry, Doreen, the call must have dropped."

"Hello, Holland," said a silky smooth voice, and Holland's heart began to flutter.

"Hi, Jonas!"

"I hear traffic sounds; are you outdoors?"

"Yes, I was taking a walk, but I'm heading home now. Are you okay?"

"For now, I'm fine. But my heart aches for you."

"Yeah, mine too," she said in a voice that came out in whimper.

"Before you return home, can you do me a favor?"

"Of course."

"Would you mind meeting me at our spot in the park?"

"I'm on my way."

"I'll be waiting for you."

CHAPTER 9

Overjoyed, Holland practically jogged to the park. She laughed to herself, realizing that she fit right in with the strange, night-time travelers that were hurrying along the streets of Frombleton.

As she grew closer to the park, she could see a figure standing near the entrance. The moon's glow streamed through tree branches and highlighted Jonas's face. She could clearly see his smooth, mocha complexion, his strong jawline, and his sumptuous, full lips. At the sight of him, her breath caught and her heart skipped several beats. Impulsively, she picked up her pace, eager to get to him...ready to leap into his arms. But instead of running, she reduced her speed, and began walking very slowly and carefully, as if any rapid movements might cause her elusive lover to evaporate before her eyes.

⊕ ⊕ ⊕

Jonas had been waiting for Holland at their favorite spot, but when he detected her enticingly sweet scent, he walked to the park's entrance to meet her. Eyes closed blissfully, he inhaled her fragrance, filling his nostrils until he was almost intoxicated with pleasure. The soft tread of her footsteps announced her arrival, and his eyes opened in excitement. The sight of her sent a rush of love swirling through him. Briefly forgetting the woeful reason he'd asked her to meet him, he made swift strides toward her.

"Oh, Jonas," Holland whispered, her gaze lingering on his face.

He enfolded her in a tight embrace, murmuring her name over and over. "I missed you. I wish we could be together like this forever," he said, his fingers stroking her hair.

Holland clung to him with her cheek pressed against his chest. "Just hold me," she said softly, melting into him as his arms tightened around her. After a few moments, he loosened his embrace, and Holland looked into his eyes. "We've been through so much together, and yet we're always saying goodbye. I love you, Jonas; why does it have to be this way?"

"I love you, too. With all my heart, and I'm sorry. I never intended to hurt you," he soothed, his long fingers caressing her face.

"Then stop hurting me," she said in a pained voice. "We've said goodbye so many times, and I never know when or *if*, I'm ever going to see you again. It's unbearable. I can't even smile when we're apart."

"I've been doing the best that I can, but my life is such a nightmare."

"So is mine! I lost my best friend; the girls at my prominent new school were only pretending to like me so they could steal my blood, and I've recently learned that there's an army of vampires plotting against the people of Frombleton."

"Let's walk," Jonas suggested quietly. Holland nodded, and he guided her away from the park entrance. They walked in solemn silence for a few minutes, his arm draped over her shoulder and hers wrapped around his waist.

Holland came to a stop, and Jonas gazed at her questioningly. "What's wrong?" he asked.

"Everything's wrong. What are we doing, Jonas? When am I going to start seeing you more regularly?"

"I don't know."

"You don't know?" Shaking her head, she struggled to fight tears. "You could at least keep your word and call me like you say you will. You have no idea how it feels to be in a permanent state of waiting—waiting to hear from you; waiting to see you again. You have no idea how much it hurts."

"I'll call more often, but I can't promise anything else."

"Why not?"

"I'm not suitable to be yours or *anyone's* boyfriend. Not in my condition." He inhaled a slow breath. "I love you, Holland. I swear I do, but it's best if you start seeing other people. You know…someone who can be there for you…not someone who's cursed."

"Are you breaking up with me?" she asked in a shrill voice.

He nodded grimly. "I think it would be best if you moved on."

"I can't believe this…you asked me to come here so you could break up with me? That's cruel, Jonas."

Now Jonas's eyes glimmered with tears. "It would have been cowardly of me to tell you over the phone, and that's why I wanted to meet with you, face to face. I wanted to tell you that I'll never love anyone the way I love you."

"How can you say that?" she cried, her voice going up several pitches.

"Because it's true. I love you, Holland, more than you'll ever know."

"Love shouldn't feel like this. Do you have any idea how many scars you've left on my heart?" She touched her chest and whimpered as tears streamed down her face. Sobbing softly, her shoulders began to shake.

Gathering her in his arms, Jonas murmured, "Hurting you is the last thing I ever wanted to do, but being the way I am, I can't figure out any other alternative."

"But I accept you as you are...you know that," she said, wiping her eyes and sniffling.

"I don't want to be accepted like this. I'm an abomination, Holland, but I've made peace with the monster I am," he said in a calm voice, the features of his gorgeous face arranged in an expression of serenity.

"You're not a monster," she said, shaking her head. "How can you say that?"

Jonas leaned in close, looking Holland in the eye. "I can say it, because it's true. The voodoo priestess was my last hope, and she couldn't help me. Not only was she unable to reverse the spell, she was terrified and repulsed by me. Mamba Mathilde called me vile and evil. She pleaded with me to leave Haiti before my evil spread throughout my homeland." His passive expression morphed into a slight frown. "I've lost all hope for my redemption," he said, releasing a sigh.

"You can't give up, Jonas. Just because Mamba Mathilde couldn't help doesn't mean that the curse is irrevocable."

"There's nowhere else for me to turn, and now I've decided to focus on caring for the misfortunate creatures that I've unwittingly created."

"But..." Holland inclined her head to one side, looking at Jonas in bewilderment. "What misfortunate creatures?"

"The flesh-eaters, like me."

"Where'd they come from?"

"That's a mystery that I hope to unravel. These creatures are worse off than I am. They've lost every trace of their humanity. They've lost their ability to communicate. They're wild and ravenous and no longer possess any rational thought. Their bodies are ripped and torn carcasses that are rapidly decaying." Jonas winced as he thought about the two creatures he'd led out of the cornfield: the woman with the open cavity in her stomach and the man with a series of bites and gouges, and a foot that was awkwardly twisted. "If you saw them, you'd be horrified. They're dead people that have risen and are now viciously feeding on living beings."

Holland shivered involuntarily. "They sound even worse than vampires."

"Yes, I believe they are. Vampires can be reasoned with…even outwitted, but these creatures have lost their capacity for intelligent thought. And sadly, I think that I'm to blame for all the devastation they're causing."

"I don't understand. Why are you taking responsibility? Maybe a spell has been cast on all of them."

"I feel connected to them," Jonas confided. He clasped Holland's hands. "While in Haiti," he said softly, "I could hear their cries in my mind—I could feel their anguish. I knew they were calling me, pleading for guidance. I don't know how they became the way they are, but I know instinctively that somehow I'm the cause of these dreadful, yet pitiful beings. They're multiplying fast, and if I don't intervene…their rampage against humans will be tragic."

"Are they here in Frombleton?" Holland asked in a fearful voice.

"No, not yet. But they're growing close. I can feel them."

"What's your plan? How are you going to stop them?"

"I've contained two of them—confined them in a place where they can't hurt anyone. But the problem is, there are more of them—many more, and they're spreading out to bordering towns. I've got to find a way to draw them to me."

"Drawing them to you sounds dangerous. Have you considered

that they may not want your guidance? I mean, suppose they band together and turn on you?"

Jonas shook his head. "That won't happen. I feel no more threatened than a parent feels in the presence of his child. I'm going to figure out a way to communicate with them, and teach them to survive as I do."

"There has to be a simpler way." Holland looked off in thought for a moment, and then returned her attention to Jonas. "If your spell was broken, what do you think would happen to these creatures? Would they still be rampaging against humans?"

"I don't think so. I believe their dark hunger would finally be satisfied, and they'd meet the peaceful death they were denied."

"That's the answer, then. We have to break that terrible spell."

"Holland, there's no use—"

"Voodoo isn't the only magic in the world," Holland said sharply. "My magic is powerful, Jonas. Let me help you."

"But...you're only a novice, Holland. You're still learning. The evil spell that's been cast upon me is unalterable. It's a miserable fate, but you have to accept it, as I have."

"I can't."

"You have no choice."

"Yes, I do. Do you remember what you told my mother when she warned you that the witches at Stoneham had strong powers?"

"No, I don't recall."

"You told her that nothing is stronger than the power of love. Do you remember saying that?"

A smile flickered across his face. "Yes, I remember now."

"That's how I feel about the curse you're under. I can break the spell because nothing is stronger than the power of love."

"Holland," he uttered, his voice lilting in protest.

"I knew that you would rescue me from those Stoneham witches, and you did. Now, I need you to believe in me the way that I believed in you."

"Sounds fair," Jonas said quietly, and then lowered his head and covered Holland's mouth with his.

She pressed her palms against the sides of his head, and parted her lips, kissing him more deeply than ever before.

CHAPTER 10

radley woke up with a start. He flung the sheet from his bare chest, and for a moment he thought he was in his smartly furnished condo. But the crisp, lavender-scented sheets at home would never hold the scent of mold and dust that now drifted up to his nostrils.

Eyes wandering, he saw the aged wallpaper and the old-fashioned furniture, and he realized that once again, he'd awakened in the outdated hotel from hell. Waking up like this was becoming a recurring nightmare. Panic-stricken, his breath emerging in quick gasps, he shot a glance at the other twin bed, and found it empty. "Tessa!" he called out, his voice cracking in desperation.

Violent memories surfaced when he noticed his crumpled suit jacket hanging over the side of the bed. The shredded fabric pieces of his blood-stained shirt were scattered around the floor. Bradley jumped to his feet; he quickly threw on the crinkled jacket and fled the room.

"Tessa!" he shouted, running along the long, darkened hallway, and twisting doorknobs that led into empty rooms.

What had those demons done to his daughter? Was she still alive or had they completely drained her?

Recalling that he'd been viciously bitten by several vampires, he stopped cold, his panicked fingers examining himself for injuries. Amazingly, his wrists and arms were smooth and unblemished.

Confused, he ran his hand over his neck and then his shoulders, feeling for the gouging wounds that the crazed, acrobatic vampire called Chaos had inflicted with his claws. But the gashes in his shoulders were no longer there, and the terrible pain was also gone.

Flooded with relief, Bradley wondered if he was going insane and had perhaps imagined it all. Tessa was probably safe and sound at home, and a call to Nicole would confirm that their daughter was all right. Searching for his cell phone, he patted his pockets, and then groaned in distress when he remembered that one of the female vampires had snatched it from him while he was trying to get help for Tessa. *This madness is real*, he solemnly admitted. Feeling desperate, he fell against a wall, panting and raking his fingers through his hair as he tried to figure out his next move.

Sadly, he didn't know what to do. He'd gone from being an indignant and entitled hotshot attorney to a man teetering on the brink of sanity in a short time span.

A distant scream from a floor below caused the hairs on the back of his neck to rise. "Oh, God, Tessa!" Bradley cried in a voice thick with dread. He skidded down several flights of stairs, yelling his daughter's name. The screams grew closer when he reached the main level.

From the corner of his eye, he saw a flash of movement and then felt an eerie chill as a pair of icy lips brushed against his cheek. "Looking for someone, Counselor?" a voice hissed in his ear.

Bradley recoiled from the lips that were as cold as death. "I'm trying to find my daughter," he croaked. "I'll do whatever you people want; but please, stop torturing her."

"Good to know," said Lisette, her blue eyes sparkling bright in the dark corridor. "Let's have a talk with Elson, shall we?" She prodded Bradley forward with a sharpened fingernail that was poked in the center of his back.

Next, he was shoved into a large conference room, and the startling scene inside reminded him of a Nazi concentration camp. There were about fifty or more people—vampire captives—that looked forlorn and hopeless as they stood in several long lines, trembling in fear as they waited to donate blood. A crew of vampires was busy at work, siphoning their blood into pint-sized plastic bags.

Bradley recognized numerous people by name. The Stoddard family was there, but he didn't see their high school-aged daughter, Sophia. And there was Tanya Fluegfelder, the pretty librarian with a luxurious mane of red hair. The Vasquez family also stood in line, and Chaela, the oldest daughter, looked gaunt and un-kempt in a wrinkled, cheerleading uniform.

As he glanced around the room, he winced when he met the frantic gazes of Amy Horsheck and her husband, Derek. Amy was a paralegal at his law firm, and Bradley despised being seen in such a vulnerable position by one of his employees.

"Where's Tessa?" Bradley asked again.

"She's resting and recovering." Lisette smiled tauntingly and tightened the clutch on his arm.

"I heard her screaming; why are you people still tormenting her?"

"That wasn't your daughter's screams; you heard the pained howls of stupid rebels who resisted Elson's policies."

Bradley swallowed hard. "What are his policies?"

"You humans have been given specific days and times to come in and have your blood drawn. Those who complain or protest in any manner will suffer tremendous agony, and those who comply will enjoy the simplicity of a needle's prick and will lose a reasonable amount of blood each week."

"That's preposterous! There are laws that protect human rights. How long do you think you can get away with this lunacy before law enforcement gets involved?"

Lisette smiled and nodded toward the doorway, and Bradley could hardly believe his eyes. Crossing the threshold was a uniformed police officer, forcibly dragging in a screaming, rebellious woman, a former client of his named Heather Campbell.

"Please," Heather said. "I can't give blood; I have low blood sugar. I'll get sick if—"

"Keep it moving, Heather," the policeman said in a gruff voice.

"This is so unfair; I'm not well, and you're treating me like I'm a criminal."

"Make sure you get here on time next week; if I have to pick you up again, you're not going to like the outcome."

Strolling behind the cop and chatting casually were two detectives that Bradley knew pretty well: Walsh and Canelli. He knew them to be tough, hardworking cops—good guys! Why was the police force aiding vampires?

Bradley tried to get Walsh's attention, but the detective barely gave him a glance. Walsh was fully engaged in a conversation with a provocatively dressed young woman, an obvious vampire, with shrewd dark eyes and a wicked smile.

Next, he tried his luck with Walsh's partner, Canelli, giving him a beseeching look. Canelli also ignored him, his eyes excitedly sweeping the room that was crowded with terror-stricken people. Canelli glanced at Walsh and gave the 'thumbs up' gesture, as if the citizens of Frombleton had willingly come out in droves to support a good cause.

The uniformed cop shoved Heather to the back of the line.

"Please, no," Heather pleaded, taking faltering steps toward the policeman.

"Get back in line; I'm not going to repeat myself," the cop said tersely. "Either stay in line and give blood of your own accord or join the siphoning party down the hall."

Heather's eyes grew wide in fright. "I'll stay in line," she responded quickly, and then straightened her shoulders as if summoning courage.

"Siphoning party! Good one—that's real funny, officer." Canelli laughed heartily.

Bradley figured the detectives and the uniformed cop couldn't possibly understand the grave situation the residents of Frombleton were in. "Detective Canelli, you have to do something," he said desperately. He pointed to the vampire team that was tasked with withdrawing blood. "They aren't medical professionals. They're not even real people—they're vampires!

"They have my daughter, Tessa. She's somewhere in this hell-hole, and she's badly injured. You have to find her," Bradley said imploringly.

A vampire wearing a ten-gallon hat withdrew a needle from the librarian's delicate arm, and instead of applying a cotton ball and adhesive to the pierced skin, the vampire extended a dark tongue and licked the dots of blood that dribbled from the tiny puncture. The librarian recoiled and uttered a fearful sound.

The cowboy vampire tipped his hat, winked at the librarian, and then gave her a fang-toothed smile. "I'll see you same time next week, ma'am," he said in a pronounced Southern drawl.

Her head hung miserably, Tanya Fluegfelder clutched her jacket around her lithe body and hurried out of the conference room.

"Next in line!" the vampire barked impatiently. A senior citizen hobbled forward, pushing up the sleeve of his sweater, eyes blinking in fear as he prepared to have his blood drawn.

"You're in the wrong line, old-timer," the vampire advised with a smirk.

Canelli chuckled when he noticed that aside from the old man, the cowboy vampire's line was made up of mostly attractive young women. "Hey, Travis, you can't discriminate and stick it to the hot chicks only. You have to get blood from everyone we rounded up," Canelli teased.

"The sixty-five-and-over crowd belong in the doom room, per Elson's orders," Travis informed.

The mere mention of Elson's name wiped the smirk off Canelli's face. Walsh pulled his attention away from the vampire girl he was chatting with and arranged his features into a serious expression. "I'll escort the old guy down the hall," Walsh offered.

Upon realizing that officers of the law were in cahoots with the vile, vampires, Bradley's chest began to squeeze around his heart. Glancing around in desperation, he spotted the faded letters of the exit sign. He yearned to break free of Lisette's grasp and make a run for it, but he couldn't leave the miserable hotel without Tessa.

"I'm on my way to the doom room," Lisette said. "Come on, Pops; you're going with me."

"Where're we going?" the old man asked fearfully.

Lisette's face hardened. "No questions; do as I say!"

The old man shuffled alongside Lisette, while Bradley tried to walk with as much dignity as a shirtless man wearing a tattered suit coat could manage.

CHAPTER 11

L isette led Bradley and the old man down the molding corridor, and Bradley could hear tortured cries as he neared the notorious 'doom room.' Though he braced himself for the worst, he was ill-prepared for the nightmarish events that awaited him on the other side of the double doors.

The doom room was significantly larger than the conference room where the blood drive was occurring. There were approximately twenty people inside this room—women, men, and children, and many were bleeding from punctures on their necks and wrists. The atmosphere was frantic with some families huddled together and sobbing softly, while others wept openly as they pleaded to go home. Vampires wearing illicit smiles on their blood-stained lips slipped in and out of the room in pairs and trios.

A female vampire dressed in a body-hugging, black lace gown, began to entertain the petrified hostages with a horribly, discordant melody. Fixing her attention on a woman and her petrified little boy, the vampire inched close and then suddenly snatched the trembling child away from its mother.

"Let go of my son," the mother shrieked, rushing to her son's aid. Two snarling male vampires immediately grabbed the hysterical woman, and roughly restrained her.

The chubby little boy, a toddler, no older than two, was wearing a white Old Navy T-shirt, a red hoodie, and neatly-cuffed jeans. The little boy cried as he was lifted in the air and cradled in the female vampire's arms.

Singing a morbid lullaby in a voice that sounded rusty and terrifying, the vampire woman twirled and danced around the room. The boy thrashed and shrieked frantically, and the vampire began spinning and spinning at a speed so fast and feverish, the child became too dizzy to scream.

Eyes filled with horror, the boy's mother screeched, "Put him down. Please! You're scaring him!" She fought to break the vampires' hold, but was unable to. Hopeless, she broke down and wept.

At the conclusion of the ghoulish song, the vampire woman bared her fangs, and then fiendishly buried her face in the child's plump neck. Crying for his mother, the little boy kicked and twisted in the vampire's cold grip. With her teeth embedded in the boy's tender flesh, the vampire moaned and gurgled, making a terrible, gritty sound. She slurped and fed greedily, all the while stroking the boy's fluffy curls with her yellowed claws. Withdrawing her fangs briefly, the vampire stared at the horrified mother of the child. "His blood is so sweet; absolutely delicious," she taunted, lowering her eyelids almost blissfully while streams of blood trickled down her chin. Resuming her feast, the vampire switched to the opposite side of the boy's neck.

Shaking her head violently, the mother watched helplessly as her child's body finally went limp. "Stop it, please—you're killing my son!"

But the vampire didn't stop feeding until the child uttered a final strangled gasp, his rosy complexion now changed to a deathly blue-gray. She ruthlessly dropped the lifeless little body from her arms, and it tumbled to the floor with a sickening clunk.

The male vampires released the mother, and she ran to her son, screaming piercingly. Calling his name, she shook him harshly. Unable to revive him, she pressed her lips against his and tried to breathe life back into his body. But her efforts were in vain. The child was as still as stone and before long, the mother's screams turned into mournful sobs.

Taking over the entertainment segment of the horror show, Chaos entered the room doing front flips, and then, as if performing to rousing music, he transitioned into a few dance moves that were followed by a series of wild somersaults, handstands, and aerial cartwheels. Instead of wowing the crowd, his frenzied jumble of acrobatics evoked startled gasps as baffled spectators scurried out of his way.

Smiling with approval, Lisette applauded the circus-like performance. "I bet you've worked up quite a thirst." She nodded toward the old man. "Feel free to drain him," she said with a smile on her face as she callously shoved the old man toward Chaos.

"Don't come near me," the old man shouted, wielding his cane like a weapon. "I don't want to be in here; let me go back to that other room," he shouted, gazing at Lisette pleadingly.

Lisette shook her head. "Sorry, Pops. Elson likes fresh blood, and yours has probably gone sour."

"Blood is blood; age doesn't make a difference," the old man objected, his eyes glistening with tears.

"Elson will know the difference. He doesn't like blood that's close to its expiration date," Lisette said sharply.

"Please. I don't wanna die like that," the old man whined and pointed to the blood-drained little boy who was now sprawled out on his weeping mother's lap.

Lisette shook her head. "Face it, Pops; your time is up."

The old man appealed to Bradley. "You're a lawyer...You

represented my great-nephew in a criminal case a few years ago. My nephew was guilty as sin, but you convinced that jury to acquit him. Can't you reason with these vampire folks on my behalf? I'll pay you," he offered with a smile that was more like a grimace.

Bradley didn't answer. He glanced downward, fiddling with the buttons on his jacket so he didn't have to meet the old man's gaze. This was obviously no courtroom and he was powerless here. Chaos and two other vampires surrounded the old man and seized his arms, causing his cane to fly out of his hand and clank against the wall. The trio of vampires attached their hungry mouths to his pulse points and sank their teeth in, and the room became filled with the old man's howls. As his life flow ebbed, the man's screams died down to croaks and gasps, and Bradley was grateful when the man's pitiful cries finally ended. There was a brief moment of silence, and then there was the sound of the old man's brittle bones cracking when his body hit the floor.

Bradley noticed several people sidling up to the vampires in the back of the room. He couldn't hear what they were saying, but from the frantic look in their eyes, and their desperate gestures, he got the impression that they were attempting to strike deals that would allow them to get out of the execution room into the more civilized environment where the volunteer donors were having their blood drawn.

He couldn't blame them. The gory violence…the moaning and weeping inside the doom room was frightening and un-bearable. And the dreadful vampire singing and bizarre acrobatics was like being forced to endure entertainment from the pit of hell.

It was time for Bradley to strike a deal also. "Is my daughter still alive?" he asked Lisette.

"I guess," Lisette said with a shrug.

"I need to speak with Elson at once."

"He's busy."

"It's urgent. Can you pass on the message that I'm more than ready to handle his real estate deal? Tell him that I can begin the paperwork this evening if he'd like." Bradley offered a pained smile.

CHAPTER 12

Holland waved when Rebecca Pullman pulled into the mall parking lot. After easing into the passenger's seat, Holland could see the tension etched on Rebecca's face.

"Are you okay, Rebecca?"

"No, I'm not. First of all, you're not supposed to be out at night, young lady; and secondly, I left an important meeting to bring you the book." She twisted around and retrieved from the back seat, the worn leather book of spells that had been in Tami's possession at Stoneham Academy. "Couldn't this have waited until tomorrow?"

Holland fidgeted. She couldn't tell Rebecca that she was desperate to find a spell that would remove the curse from Jonas. Rebecca was so certain that Jonas's condition was unalterable; she would have considered Holland's attempts to reverse the spell as a complete waste of time.

"I asked you to meet me here because I didn't want Mom to know about the book." Holland made a face. "You know how she is; she might not be able to resist snooping and trying to work a little magic. I wanted to have the book because...well, I realize that I need more than the tidbits of knowledge I'm discovering instinctively. You know what I mean? I need more structured training—like I was getting at Stoneham."

"That's exactly what I tried to tell you, Holland. The Book of

Spells has its value, but it won't replace the knowledge that can be acquired in a structured learning environment."

"I know, and I'm thinking about returning to Stoneham next year, but in the meantime, I figured I'd do some independent studying at home."

Rebecca's face lit up. "That's wonderful, Holland—a wise decision. I was trained at Stoneham and you won't get a better education anywhere in the world." She placed a hand over Holland's. "What you went through at Stoneham was traumatizing; I get that, but I want you to know there are measures in place to prevent practitioners of dark magic from infiltrating those hallowed halls ever again."

Rebecca handed Holland the book that was wrapped in purple silk. "This book contains ancient wisdom. Respect it and use it only for good."

"I will," Holland said. A tingle ran up Holland's arm when she ran her hand across the aged leather cover. "Thank you, Rebecca."

"You're welcome. I have to get back to the meeting." Anxiety furrowed her brows.

"Is something wrong?"

Rebecca gave a long sigh. "The vampires have a new leader. We hear he's shrewd and ruthless, and he's clandestinely organizing all the vampires in the area. He's also using foolish humans to lure others to the vampires' nesting place. If we witches don't find a way to stop them, the citizens of Frombleton could all become blood slaves."

"What can I do to help?"

Rebecca shook her head. "You're too valuable to risk putting in harm's way. If things get out of control, we're going to have to move you and your mother out of Frombleton and take you to a safe house at an undisclosed location."

Holland frowned, and shouted in her mind, *I can't leave Jonas!*

She said aloud, "Those bloodsuckers can't run me out of town."

"You're a rare witch, Holland, and it's our duty to protect you."

"I know. It's just that it seems so cowardly to hide out while everyone else is actively combating the vampires."

"We're getting ahead of ourselves. If we find their nest, we can destroy them while they sleep during the day."

"I may be able to get that answer for you."

"How would you be able to obtain such top-secret information?"

"There's a girl at school who claims to party with the vamps. She says she knows them personally."

Rebecca shook her head, adamantly. "No, you stay away from her; she may be one of the pawns they use to lure humans."

"I don't think so. She's come to realize how cruel and violent they are, and she's been wearing a cross around her neck—"

Rebecca made a scoffing sound. "How very original. Sorry, but a crucifix won't protect her."

"It's silver, though...they hate silver, don't they?"

"Large amounts of silver can bind them, but a cross and a thin chain won't be effective at all."

"I'll talk to her at school tomorrow...find out where they nest. I won't let her lure me anywhere and I won't go anywhere near her at nightfall. Are you comfortable with that?"

"Not really."

"I have to do something to help destroy the vamps."

"Be careful, Holland. Call me as soon as you get the information."

⊕ ⊕ ⊕

In her bedroom with the door locked, Holland turned the delicate pages of The Book of Spells. The book itself seemed to possess so much energy, she could feel electrical currents coursing through her fingertips. A cursory glance indicated that most of the spells were rituals that didn't require gathering a bunch of weird ingredients and nothing needed to be stirred in a cauldron. Experimenting with one of the spells, she lit a white candle, envisioned Jonas's face, and quietly recited a Latin incantation. She had no idea what the Latin words meant and hoped she was pronouncing them right.

After a few minutes, Holland got into a rhythm, and the sound of her voice was hypnotic, relaxing her until her body became so light, she was barely aware of it. It was a peaceful state, and Jonas's face was emblazoned on her mind, as clearly as if he were physically standing before her. She stared into his eyes, and as if they were actually face to face, she saw her own image reflected in his eyes.

Her ringing cell phone jolted her back to reality. "Hello?"

"Hey, it's Jonas. How are you?"

"I'm good. Surprised to hear from you."

"I told you I would make an effort to be a better boyfriend," he said with a little laugh. "What were you doing; did I catch you at a bad time?"

"Uh, I'm in my room, and I was actually working on a spell, you know, a hex-removing spell." She chuckled nervously. "I don't expect to be successful right away, but um…I'm curious…has anything changed? Do you feel different at all?"

"No, everything's pretty much the same. My senses are still heightened. And even though I've taught myself to control the hunger, it's still there. I appreciate what you're trying to do, Holland…I really do, but I'm not getting my hopes up."

"I'm going to keep trying," she said stubbornly.

"And I'm going to enjoy living in the moment. I called because I was wondering if you had plans for tomorrow night."

"No...why?"

"I'd like to take you out."

"Like on a date?"

"Yes."

"Wow! Sure. Where are we going?"

"Maybe we could check out a movie—is that okay?"

"Yeah, I'd love to."

"Okay, then. Do you want to meet at the mall tomorrow—around seven?"

"Perfect."

CHAPTER 13

The clock on the dashboard read: 10:23. "If we were in school, I'd be in chemistry class," Jarrett observed.

Sitting in the passenger's seat of his Durango, Sophia Stoddard scowled. "I'd be in boring English Lit. School sucks; I hate it."

You suck! He didn't like Sophia at all, but his vampire girlfriend, Ismene had paired them together to canvass Frombleton neighborhoods during daytime hours, and so he had no choice but to put up with her. "Why're you complaining? You don't have to go back to school if you don't want to."

"I don't think the truancy officers would agree with that."

"Screw the truancy officers. What are they gonna do—lock you up? I don't think so."

"You have a point, Sloan. With my parents having to obey the vamps and having the cops on my side, I'm like...untouchable," Sophia said with cocky smile.

Jarrett slowed the SUV when he reached Greenland Meadows, a fairly new community with a collection of one- and two-story homes that featured sleek modern designs with stucco, stone, and brick exteriors. The professionally maintained lawns and outdoor spaces gave the area an eye-appealing quality. "Ready to visit some neighbors?"

Sophia shrugged indifferently. "It doesn't matter to me. As long as we reach our quota, I'm good."

After they cruised along the driveway that led into the complex, and then parked, Jarrett reached behind the seat and grabbed his backpack that was inscribed with the Frombleton Community College logo.

"Let's go get 'em, college boy," Sophia said with an obnoxious giggle.

The first house they approached was a white stucco one-story with cutesy window boxes filled with autumn flowers. A cheery blue and white welcome mat adorned the front porch, and Jarrett had the feeling that getting the signature of the cornballs that lived in this house would be easy, breezy.

Sophia pressed the doorbell and frowned excessively when instead of hearing a traditional ding-dong, there were strains of Beethoven's Fifth Symphony. "That's so lame."

"Yeah, a musical doorbell should be blasting something by Linkin Park or Green Day."

Sophia pressed the bell again. "I'd prefer Nicki Minaj or Katy Perry."

"Ugh, chick music…your taste sucks."

"What's Ismene like to listen to?" Sophia asked, an eyebrow arched.

Jarrett pondered the question, but realized he didn't know the answer. He supposed Ismene enjoyed music from her era—whenever that was. She was very secretive about her background.

The door swung open. A woman, who seemed around Jarrett's mom's age, only less stylish, leaned against the doorjamb. With thick-rimmed glasses, a bad bob haircut, and elastic-waist, Mom jeans, her appearance was a disaster. "Can I help you?" she asked with a look of surprise.

Jarrett offered a friendly smile. "Hi, there. Um, we're students at Community College and we're gathering names and addresses of Frombleton residents that think it's about time we had a children's hospital in our town."

"Oh," the woman muttered. "A children's hospital would be a good idea, I suppose."

"It sure would," Sophia piped in. "When our kids get hurt or if they're really sick, they have to be flown over two hundred miles to receive adequate pediatric care."

Jarrett dug into his backpack and pulled out a form. "If you'd sign this petition, and include your address and phone number, we'd really appreciate it."

The woman studied the petition. "You two have been very busy; you have quite a few signatures, I see."

"Yes, ma'am. Our citizens want improved health care for the kids."

"Where would the hospital be located?"

"Huh?" Jarrett's facial muscles quivered as his smile began to morph into a frown. *Just sign the damn paper, lady! You're wasting valuable time.*

Sophia quickly plastered a warm smile on her face. "The location hasn't been decided yet. Our goal is to let city officials know that we believe that children are the future."

Children are the future? Geez! So lame! Jarrett shot Sophia a hostile glance. She shrugged in response.

The woman studied the petition again. "I'm making sure there's no fine print," she said and then finally poised the pen Jarrett had given her. With her signature affixed next to her address and phone number, Jarrett and Sophia were ready to move on.

"Oh, yeah, I forgot to mention…uh, there's a meeting tonight at seven sharp."

"What sort of meeting?" The woman's mouth turned down in disapproval.

"A planning meeting and a blood drive," Jarrett said.

"I signed your petition, but I'm not interested in anything else."

"You don't have a choice." Wearing a solemn expression, Jarrett shook his head.

"Is this some sort of prank?"

"No, we're dead serious," Sophia informed. "You're expected to be at the old Lilac Hotel tonight at seven."

"The Lilac? It's been shut down for years."

"It reopened a few months ago. Look, lady, if you don't show up, you're gonna regret it."

Eyes flaming, the woman snatched open the door. "You kids are sick, and I want you to leave! I will not be threatened in my own home."

"How many people are in this household?" Sophia inquired.

"That is absolutely none of your business."

"It's best if you come clean…" Jarrett's voice trailed off as he perused her signature. "Listen, Judy Carmichael; I'm gonna give it to you straight. Have you been hearing the rumors about people being attacked by vampires?"

Judy nodded, her eyes growing wide with incredulity.

"It's not a rumor; it's true. Vamps are taking over the town. Now, what you've actually done is given your consent to donate blood."

"Are you nuts? I didn't sign any such thing," Judy bellowed.

"Yeah, you did. Now, you can do it the easy way, which means you show up at the hotel and have your blood drawn in a civilized manner. But if you decide to shirk your responsibility, your home is going to be swarming with vampires by nightfall."

Sophia wagged her finger at Judy. "And the things those vamps will do to you and your family will probably land you in the loony bin."

"Or the cemetery…without an ounce of blood left in your body. You know, like that McFadden dude," Jarrett added.

"Oh, God! You can't be serious," Judy uttered, backing away, her eyes widening into fearful circles.

"I'm very serious. Now, list the members of your household." Jarrett gave Judy a separate sheet of paper.

Judy picked up the pen with a shaky hand. She started to write, but suddenly dropped the pen. "I can't write down my children's names. I just can't." She gripped her chest.

"Okay, then. You've been warned," Jarrett said in a foreboding tone, and then he and Sophia turned to leave.

"Wait!" Judy shouted. "How about I give you my estranged husband's name? Will you take him instead of my children and me?"

"Does he reside here in Frombleton?"

Judy pressed her lips together and shook her head grimly. "No, he lives in Florida."

"Sorry, Judy. The vamps haven't branched out that far, yet."

In an act of desperation, Judy picked up the pen and tried to scratch her name off the list, but Sophia grabbed her wrist and Jarrett salvaged the paper.

"Write down the members of this household and their ages before we get rough with you," Sophia hissed.

"Okay, okay," Judy whined. She wrote down two additional names: Megan Carmichael, age 12, and Ryan Carmichael, age 11.

"See you and the kids tonight, Judy," Sophia taunted. "Don't be late."

CHAPTER 14

On the lookout for biters, Eden, Gabe, and Leroy had taken shifts throughout the night, guarding the store while Charlotte took care of Jane. Occasional biters had been spotted shuffling along the street, but it had been a relatively peaceful night, without any uprisings or attacks. Now, Leroy rested upstairs and Charlotte was asleep on a cot in the storage room.

Eden and Jane slept together on a pallet on the floor, while Gabe kept watch, drifting back and forth from the window to the chair behind the counter. With the rising sun, there was a sudden and calamitous pounding on the door. Startled, Eden bolted upright, and Jane cried out in alarm. Gabe picked up his rifle and moved to the window, motioning for Eden to take Jane to the area in the back.

"Help! Is anyone in there? Open the door!" a male voice shouted.

At the sound of the commotion, Leroy scrambled down the stairs, his gun in hand. "What's going on; are those *things* trying to get in here?"

"Let me in!" the voice demanded.

Charlotte came out of the storage room, rubbing her eyes sleepily. "That sounds like a live person."

"Probably a dang looter!" Leroy said bitterly.

"Are you in there, Leroy? Open the door; it's me…Tony!" called the voice outside.

Leroy gave an audible sigh of relief. "It's Tony—my bread delivery guy," he explained and walked toward the door.

Gabe blocked Leroy's path. "No one's making any deliveries with those biters swarming. You can't risk letting that guy in here; suppose he got bitten?"

Leroy pushed Gabe out of his way. "Tony's the nephew of Vince Cavallo, the owner of Cavallo Breads. I'm not going to leave that kid out there to get killed by those hellish creatures."

Eden handed Jane to Charlotte. "Take her in the back, please."

Charlotte nodded. Cradling Jane, she hurried past the set of double doors that led to the storage area.

Leroy squinted through the peephole of the steel door, and Gabe aimed his rifle. Eden picked up the ax that was lying next to her pallet and then eased to the front of the store. She moved in front of a boarded window and peered between the slats.

Leroy pulled away from the peephole and gazed at Gabe and Eden with anger flaring in his eyes. "Put those weapons down. I have twenty-twenty vision, and I don't see any bite marks on Tony. He looks fine."

Eden scrutinized Tony through the window. "Yeah, he looks okay." Narrowing her eyes, she scanned to see if there was blood on his clothing. His shirt was stained with something—mud, oil—some kind of grime that she couldn't identify. "I think you should find out if he's been bitten before you let him in."

Leroy thought for a moment and then took Eden's advice. "Are you okay, Tony? Those *things* didn't bite you, did they?" he asked cautiously.

"No, I'm not bitten! Open up before these dead people scattered around the lawn start to wake up!" Tony shouted.

Leroy unlocked the door and Tony burst inside, panting and perspiring. He was a slim guy, early twenties with a trendy haircut that was packed with such an enormous amount of gel, not a hair was out of place. He wore diamond-stud earrings, a glimmering gold chain, and instead of a delivery person's uniform, he wore high-end jeans and a button-down shirt.

Upon closer inspection, Eden determined that on the front of Tony's richly-textured shirt was a crusted substance that appeared to be congealed, food stains. Although his sneakers were also splattered with unidentifiable, sticky blotches, Eden could tell from the untarnished parts that the sneakers were fairly new and expensive. Under normal circumstances, Tony was probably the type of guy that took great pride in his appearance.

Breathing hard and looking shell-shocked, Tony fell against the wall. "Ohmigod, I can't believe what's happening out there. I was making a delivery at Gordon's Restaurant—"

"This morning?" Leroy inquired with a hopeful look that perhaps some parts of town were functioning normally.

"No, everything's shut down. People are either hiding in their homes or they're trying to get out of town. I've been on the run from those crazies since yesterday afternoon. I was out making my deliveries, when suddenly all hell broke loose. I couldn't make it back to my truck, so I had to hide." He shook his head, bitterly recalling his ordeal. "I had to hide behind cars and inside abandoned houses like a sniveling punk! But, I didn't have a choice. This whole area is overrun with those crazies, and I've been out in the streets ducking and dodging them for almost twenty-four hours." He cut an eye at the boards that covered the windows, and then glanced downward at the weapons lined against the wall. "I guess you folks have been battling those crazies, too. What do you think is causing people to go wild?"

"We don't know," Gabe said. "All we can do is work together to keep them from sinking their teeth into any us. Once you're bitten, you turn into one of them."

Tony wiped perspiration from his face, and then nodded. "Yeah,

I know. I've seen it happen. I wonder if there's something poisonous in the water. I mean, what else could affect an entire town? Men, women…even kids, they've all gone bananas… acting liked crazed cannibals. People I do business with…decent people…they've all changed. And it's nasty, man. Their faces and bodies are gouged and bloody. They've got drool running out of their mouths. And they're tearing into anybody within reach, biting and viciously ripping people to shreds. I can't get the images or the sounds out of my head." Tony shuddered visibly, his lips drawn into a grim, straight line.

"What about your uncle?" Leroy asked hopefully. "Mr. Cavallo knows powerful people. I bet he can tell us what's going on."

"I tried to call Uncle Vince, you know, to warn him…but my phone's been acting screwy. I can't get a signal."

Leroy grunted in displeasure. "Did you notice any police cruisers while you were out there? I couldn't get them on the phone, and I've been trying to figure out what the heck the police are doing while the citizens are running around, mauling each other to death."

Tony made a scoffing sound. "Yeah, the cops are out there, but they've joined in the madness, gnawing on the citizens they're supposed to serve and protect."

"The police are in on it, too!" Leroy slapped his thigh in disbelief and aggravation. "I guess we're lucky the TV's still working, but a lot of good the blasted thing is doing. I can't get anything except a dark screen when I click to local stations. National news channels are reporting the Dow Jones Industrial Average, foreign affairs, and talking politics as usual. They haven't mentioned a word about the catastrophe in our little town."

"Is it okay to come out now?" Charlotte called from the storage room.

"Yeah, come on out, Charlotte," Gabe answered.

Eyeing Tony suspiciously, Charlotte emerged from the back. She patted Jane comfortingly as she stood next to Eden.

"Charlotte, this is Tony; he's a friend of Leroy's," Eden introduced.

"Where are my manners?" Leroy said. "Tony, meet Eden, Gabe, and Charlotte. Charlotte's been babysitting for their little daughter," Leroy added and Eden didn't bother to correct him. She was busy sizing up Tony, trying to figure out if he would be an asset or a liability to their group. It was hard to tell. The way he was shaking and seemingly close to falling apart, she suspected he might be as useless as Charlotte when it came to warfare with the biters.

"How close are the biters?" Gabe asked Tony.

"Too close, man," Tony said in a quavering voice. "They're moving around in packs, breaking into businesses along Pelham Avenue and other main streets."

Gabe shared a look with Eden. "Pelham Avenue? Isn't that where the nearest gas station is?"

Tony rubbed a hand roughly over his face. "Yeah, there's a Texaco station on Pelham, but nobody's buying gas. The lot is filled with abandoned cars and crazies roaming around looking for fresh meat. They're moving slow and clumsy-like, but it's only a matter of time before they find their way here." He gestured toward the front lawn, and then glanced at Leroy. "Are those your customers sprawled out in the yard?"

"I don't know those folks," Leroy muttered contemptuously.

Tony peeked through the slats and shook his head ominously. "They're not going to stay dead, you know. Dead people are rising up and terrorizing the living. They've been branching out into residential neighborhoods. People have been packing up and trying to leave town, but most don't make it to the main highway. I've seen those crazies leaping on cars and bashing in windows, and dragging out victims to feed on. They're eating folks alive!"

Charlotte groaned. "Jesus! We're already spooked; do you have to be so graphic?" She began rocking the baby and patting her back, as if Jane needed to be comforted from Tony's disturbing report.

Gabe set his rifle down. "Those dead folks on the lawn won't be getting up again. All it takes is a blow to the head, and they're done."

"No, shit! A shot to the head kills 'em for good?" Tony asked excitedly.

Gabe nodded. "Problem is, we only have three guns and one of them is out of ammo. We're pretty secure in here, but if they find a way to get in, we're gonna have to get close and fight 'em off with those." Gabe inclined his head toward the items he and Leroy had brought out of the garage.

Tony visibly cringed. "No way! I'm not getting close to those crazies!"

Eden felt a surge of annoyance. "What are you going to do if they try to break in here? Are you gonna run behind the counter and hide?" Eden said with contempt.

Tony opened his mouth to defend himself, but giving in to exhaustion, he grabbed his stomach and slid down the wall until he was seated on the floor with his knees drawn into his chest.

"What's wrong, Tony?" Leroy asked.

"My ulcers are killing me, and my medicine is in the glove compartment of the truck."

"I'll get you a glass of milk—you know, to coat your stomach," Leroy offered and hurried to the dairy case to get Tony some milk. In a flash, Leroy was back with a pint of milk, handing it to Tony.

Groaning miserably, one hand clutched his tummy, and Tony reached for the container of milk with the other. "It happened so fast," he murmured. "One minute, I was handing the head cook at Gordon's the delivery of sourdough and Italian bread, and the next minute, I heard someone holler. I whipped around and couldn't believe what I was seeing. The dishwasher dude and a female cook were fighting. Violently! Going for the jugular! The dishwasher gouged out the cook's right eye, and even with a bloody eye, dangling down her face and hanging by a thread, she was still fighting. She yanked the dishwasher toward her, and with one vicious chomp, she ripped off the dude's nose! In split seconds, the entire kitchen was in chaos, with workers savagely scratching and biting each other.

"I ran out the back door, intending to run to my truck. But just that fast, people who were leisurely walking the streets were being attacked and mauled like animals. I scrambled inside a Dumpster that was on the side of the restaurant, and from a tiny opening, I watched the carnage. I watched in disbelief as dead people came back to life and immediately began prowling around and attacking human beings."

Eden nodded and looked from Tony's shirt down to his sneakers. The Dumpster revelation accounted for the food stains on his clothing.

"How long did you have to hide in that Dumpster?" Charlotte asked with a frown.

Tony shrugged. "I don't know…too long. Finally, the hoard of crazies started to move away from the vicinity of the restaurant. That's when I took a chance and climbed out of the Dumpster. I ran to my truck, and was about to open the door, when I caught a glimpse of something moving. There were three or four of 'em—in the back of the truck with the bread—chowing down on—"

"They eat bread?" Charlotte inquired, astounded.

"No, they were chowing down on Flossie," Tony said, shaking his head solemnly.

"Who's Flossie?" Leroy wanted to know.

"A homeless woman. Whenever I make deliveries at Gordon's, I give the old lady a loaf of day-old bread. Somehow, she got inside my truck. I don't know if she was trying to get to the bread or if she was hiding from the crazies." Tony gave a harsh sigh. "What they did to the old girl was terrible. Even more horrible, she was still alive—reaching out in desperation and begging me to help her." Grimacing, Tony glanced downward and unconsciously ran his hand back and forth over his thighs. "My muscles are killing me from crouching and hiding for so many hours."

His stomach—his muscles. What a lousy coward! It seemed to Eden that Tony was making every excuse in the book to avoid helping out when the time came to go into combat against the biters.

CHAPTER 15

Jonas made an effort to look extra nice for his date with Holland, and by the time she arrived at the mall, he was looking fashionable in slim jeans, an oxford shirt, and a plaid, puffer vest. He'd arrived at the mall an hour early, and with time on his hands, he decided to browse in some of the stores. At Gap, he bought the exact outfit the mannequin in the display window was wearing.

"You look awesome," Holland complimented.

"So do you," he replied and gave her quick kiss. "Is there anything in particular you want to see?"

"Doesn't matter; I'm happy being with you," she said, reaching for his hand as they walked toward the movie complex.

They checked the movies that were playing and decided on a romantic comedy. Looking at the show times, Holland scowled. "There's an hour-and-a-half wait."

"We can see something else," Jonas suggested, scanning the various featured films.

"Actually, I don't mind waiting. We can stop by the arcade to kill time. Do you like video games?"

"No," Jonas said sharply. "I'm not interested in the arcade."

Holland gave him a quizzical look. "Okay, it was just a suggestion; we can do something else."

"I'm sorry for raising my voice; I didn't mean to. It's just that

I went to the arcade with Zac and it brings back terrible memories."

"No problem; I'm not crazy about video games, anyway. Hey, I'm suddenly starving; let's get something to…" Holland's voice trailed off and she looked at Jonas with embarrassment. "I'm sorry. I forgot about, uh…"

"My diet," he filled in with a wry smile.

"Yeah; sorry about that."

"It's okay. I can sit inside a restaurant without flipping out or anything," he said, laughing.

"But it's not fair for you to sit and watch me eat."

"I'll be fine," he reassured, noticing that the various aromas floating from the food court weren't making him nauseous like they had the last time he'd been at the mall. He supposed he was adapting to the environment.

"The mall is usually a lot more crowded in the evening. I wonder where everyone is tonight."

"I like that the mall's not hectic and jam-packed."

"Yeah, me too, but it's weird that there's such a sparse crowd tonight." She wanted to talk to Jonas about the vampires, but decided he had enough problems of his own to deal with.

As Jonas and Holland drifted toward the food court, Jonas detected a pleasant scent that stood out from the various eateries as well as the mixture of human scents. He spotted the source—a Japanese restaurant. "Do you like Japanese food?" he asked Holland.

"Never tried it, but I'm feeling adventurous."

Jonas guided Holland into the restaurant and was surprised that the combination of flavors didn't repel him—in fact, they were rather enticing.

After they were seated, the waiter announced the specials. Holland said, "I've never eaten Japanese food, so I'd better stick to something familiar—like steak."

"Be daring," the waiter encouraged. "Try a sushi appetizer."

She wrinkled her nose. "That's raw fish. Ew, I don't think so."

"Don't knock it until you've tried it." The waited winked an eye.

"Okay, I'll have the combination platter for starters."

"And you?" he asked Jonas. "Are you going to live on the edge also?"

"Yes, I'll have the same," Jonas said. Holland looked at him questioningly, and when the waiter walked away, Jonas explained, "That guy was so friendly, I felt put on the spot—like I had to order something. When the food comes, feel free to help yourself to my portions."

Their food arrived and Holland and Jonas ogled the colorful array of sushi that was placed before them. "What's that glob of green stuff?" Holland asked the waiter.

"Wasabi sauce; it's Japanese horseradish—very spicy," he warned. "You only need a little dab." He gave them a laminated placard with the images and names of the fish, and Holland and Jonas spent a few minutes identifying the sushi on their plates.

Holland tried shrimp sushi first. "Mm; it's good," she murmured, dipping the piece of shrimp into the wasabi sauce and scooping up a generous portion. The moment she bit into the shrimp, tears sprang to her eyes and she quickly wiped them away. "Oh, my God; it's super-hot!" she gasped, reaching for a glass of water and chugging it down.

"You were warned," Jonas reminded her, laughing.

"Yeah, but I didn't know it would be like fire shooting through my nostrils. That innocent-looking sauce is deceptively lethal," she said, laughing while wiping tears from her eyes.

"Back in Haiti, we enjoy spicy food. I've never tasted wasabi sauce, but I'm sure I would have an appreciation for it."

"I don't know, Jonas. It doesn't taste like hot sauce or pepper.

It's a different kind of hot." She went for another piece of sushi—tuna—and this time, skipping the wasabi sauce, she splashed it in soy sauce.

Without thinking, Jonas lifted a piece of salmon from the bed of rice and stuck it in his mouth and began to chew. Holland stared at him in disbelief. "What?" he asked, unaware that he was absently munching.

Leaning forward, she gawked at him. "You're eating food! How's it taste? Can you swallow it without gagging?"

His eyes wide with wonder, he nodded as he swallowed. "It tastes, uh, fishy."

"How do you feel? Are you nauseous?"

"No, I feel fine."

"Try another piece," Holland said enthusiastically and Jonas reached for a piece of mackerel, gobbled it down quickly, and then went for the red snapper. Holland watched him closely, her eyes glinting with a mixture of wonder and pride. "The spell worked," she whispered, awestruck.

Suddenly famished, Jonas stuffed his mouth with every piece of raw fish on his plate. "I'm sorry for behaving like a glutton, but I can't seem to get enough."

"Here, have some of mine," she said, pushing her plate toward him. "Excuse me," she called, beckoning their waiter.

The waiter came to their table and stared at Jonas, who was shoveling in raw fish with both hands. "Looks like you've become sushi lovers...or at least he has. Can I get you a couple more combo platters?"

"No, thanks. We're ready for our entrée." She gazed at the menu. "We'd both like sirloin steak."

"How would you like the steak—well-done...medium...medium-rare?"

"Medium for me, but make his rare; he likes it bloody," Holland said with an uncomfortable chuckle. She cut an eye at Jonas and saw that he'd wolfed down most of her food, leaving only rice, ginger slices, and wasabi sauce.

"Two steaks, medium and bloody coming up," the waiter said, smiling as he cleared away their plates.

"I'm not sure if I'll be able to eat steak," Jonas said worriedly. "I still don't have an appetite for cooked food—only raw meat."

"That's why I ordered it extra rare. You can scrape off the charred top. I'm crossing my fingers that you'll be able to eat the steak. Oh, Jonas, this is so exciting; you're almost back to your regular self."

"Not quite. I can hear every word spoken at that table in the back."

Holland turned around, and noticed two couples dining together in the rear of the large room. She couldn't make out their conversation, only heard indistinct murmurs and bursts of laughter.

"And the voices in my head…they're low, but I can still hear them. And when they get loud, it feels like my head is going to split in two."

"But we've made some progress, right?"

"Yes, and I thank you."

Holland leaned in and whispered, "Do you still feel the hunger… you know, for people?"

"Not really. I've been managing those cravings for a long time."

"But do you feel the urge?"

"No, not at all," he said with excitement.

"Awesome! Even if my spell didn't work completely, at least we know I'm on the right track."

"What kind of spell did you do? You know, what did it require?"

"Nothing much. It was a basic, hex-reversal ritual. All I had to do was light a candle, picture you in my mind, and recite a Latin incantation. It was easy, and I had a weird sense that we were together. In fact, you called and asked to take me out while I was in the midst of chanting the incantation."

"Hmm. I wonder if my call interfered with the spell."

"I don't think so. Your call seemed like a sign that the spell was working. At any rate, I'm going to try it again."

Jonas nodded and drifted off in thought, wondering if the creatures he'd spawned could eat raw meat, also.

The steaks arrived and after Jonas removed the crispy outside, he tore into it, closing his eyes delightfully as he chewed the bloody meat. Both Jonas and Holland wore satisfied smiles at the conclusion of their meal. "Delicious," Holland said, dabbing her lips with a napkin.

"Very satisfying," Jonas agreed. He paid the bill and then glanced at his watch. "Looks like we missed the first fifteen minutes of the movie."

"That's okay. I'm not that interested in the movie anymore. Dinner was fun and if we hadn't stopped here, we wouldn't have discovered that you're like…almost back to normal."

"Are you ready to go home?" Jonas asked as he and Holland exited the mall.

"Not really. I'm not ready for this night to end. I have Mom's car; we could go for a ride."

Jonas considered the offer. "Sounds good…but we have another option. I'm staying at the Atwell Hotel. We can hang out in my room…listen to music or watch a movie, if you'd like." He held his hands up. "Don't worry, you're safe with me; I'll be a gentleman," he assured her with a warm smile.

Jonas wrapped his arm around Holland as they walked to the

parking lot. She rested her head on his shoulder, and he breathed in her tantalizing scent. For the first time, since he'd met her, he was able to enjoy her fragrance without simultaneously fighting the urge to devour her.

Holland drove with one hand on the wheel and the other entwined with Jonas's. Love songs that seemed to be written especially for them poured from the radio. They listened in silence, squeezing each other's hand and kissing each time they stopped for a red light.

"You're so quiet; what are you thinking about?" Jonas asked Holland.

"I'm imagining all my dreams coming true."

"What do you dream of, Holland?"

"I dream of you and me...finishing high school together. Going to the same college, and getting a place together. Maybe even getting married...you know, one day...after you get your medical degree."

"I wish I were as optimistic as you, but after everything that's happened to me, being in school seems like a farfetched dream."

"But it's not farfetched at all, Jonas. You have the documents that Rebecca gave you. You could use them to enroll in school."

"I can't simply walk into high school and enroll. I need a permanent address. And a guardian," he said with a sigh.

"I can talk to Rebecca. Maybe she'd agree to act as your guardian. I'm sure she'd do it for me. After all, you rescued me. Having a witch of The First Order under her wing is important to her, so she should feel totally indebted to you for saving my life. I'm going to talk to her about getting you enrolled in school."

A troubled look crossed Jonas's face. Despite Holland's efforts, he still remained a cursed, young man. Mamba Mathilde had told him that his spirit was lost forever. He wondered if he should even hope that Holland possessed the power to restore his soul.

"I'm not ready for school, Holland."

"Why not? School is the reason you made the trip from Haiti in the first place."

Jonas realized he couldn't possibly begin anew if he left behind the battalion of flesh craving creatures that he'd spawned and that were somewhere nearby, wreaking havoc. Until he located and subdued them, he'd never have peace of mind.

"I can't commit to an education right now."

"Yes, you can."

"No!" he said firmly. "I wouldn't be able to concentrate."

At the next stop light, Holland turned and looked at him, and saw the raw pain in his eyes. "I understand, Jonas."

"Do you?"

Holland made a gesture that wasn't quite a shrug. They reached Jonas's hotel, and she pulled into the lot.

"I'm sorry, but I have to take a rain check; I don't think it's a good idea for you to come inside."

Holland winced. "Why not—what's wrong?"

"It's getting late, and I don't want to keep you out past your curfew."

She sighed. Jonas's frequent mood swings had a way of keeping her anxious and off balance.

"I'll call you tomorrow." He kissed her on the cheek.

"Please don't shut me out. I'm here for you, Jonas."

"I know," he said quietly as he got out the car. Holland could tell by the grimace on his face and the way he rubbed his temples with both hands that the voices were back, and the volume was hurting his head.

CHAPTER 16

At Leroy's Place, food and beverages were plentiful and all of Jane's needs were being met with the abundance of baby products that Leroy had on hand. Holed up together was tolerable, though no one slept easily when Tony had the duty of keeping watch. The guy was jumpy and simply didn't seem capable of keeping anyone safe. Eden marveled at the fact that Tony had survived the biters for almost twenty-four hours.

Today, the stench from the dead bodies out on the grounds of Leroy's Place had begun to drift inside the store. The smell was putrid, and was so bad, everyone had to keep their mouths and noses covered with pieces of cloth. Though Gabe and Eden were pretty sure that the death smell was what kept the biters away, the foul odor had become intolerable.

"We're going to have to get rid of those bodies," Gabe told Leroy.

Leroy frowned. "I don't want those things buried on my property."

"That wasn't the plan; there's too many to bury."

"So, what do you propose to do with 'em?"

"Pile 'em all together and burn 'em."

Brows knitted together, Leroy contemplated Gabe's suggestion. "Suppose the fumes from the fire draw those monsters to us?"

"It's a risk we're going to have to take."

"Yeah, you're right. The stench is getting unbearable. I reckon we can drag them to the back of the store, close to the wooded area. I don't wanna a big fire going up on the lawn in front of my place."

Gabe nodded. "You think Tony's feeling well enough to pitch in?"

Leroy scratched his head. "He's been complaining about his stomach again, but I'll talk to him, see if he's feeling up to snuff."

Gabe scowled. "What's he doing?"

"Upstairs, watching the news. Trying to see if there's any news about the plague that's going on in our area."

Gabe shook his head. "You coddle Tony too much."

"Tony's not cut out for hard work. He delivers bread for his uncle, and picks up money…that's it. Manual labor is not his strong suit."

"He seems like a wily sort of guy—and he knows how to get out of doing his share of work."

"Tony's a good guy. A little spoiled, that's all."

Gabe gave Leroy a sidelong glance. "During these crazy times, no one has the luxury of kicking back and relaxing; everyone has to pitch in. Who's supposed to pick up that guy's slack—Eden? She's done more than her fair share around here and I'm not going to have her lugging bodies while Tony watches TV."

"You're right. I'm gonna have a word with Tony. Let him know he's not pulling his weight around here."

"Tell Tony to stop acting like a prima donna, and to get down here and help us get rid of those rotting corpses."

⊕ ⊕ ⊕

Dragging corpses behind the store took several hours. It was hard and unpleasant labor. Due to muscle cramping, Tony's legs gave out a couple of times, and he retched every time he had to touch a dead body. Even tough-as-nails Leroy seemed on the verge of puking by the time the last body was tossed on the pile.

Gabe poured kerosene over the corpses and then torched them. Smoke billowed to the sky, but there was no sign of biters in front or behind the store.

Back inside, Gabe took Eden aside. "The coast looks clear out there. I'm considering taking a gas can and walking to that Texaco Station."

"No! We've been safe in here, but you have no way of knowing what's going on out on the streets."

"If Scary Tony could survive out there for an entire day without a weapon, I can get to Pelham Avenue and back in one piece." Gabe laughed.

Eden didn't look happy, and Gabe tilted her chin up with his finger. "Don't worry. I've got my rifle and a box full of ammo. We're getting too comfortable here, Eden. If we don't get some gas and get on our way, we may never make it to New York."

"I'm scared," she admitted. "I don't know what I'd do if something happened to you."

"Nothing is gonna happen to me."

"You said the Explorer had enough gas to make it to the gas station; I'd feel a lot better if you were inside a vehicle—you know, with glass and metal protecting you."

Gabe scowled. "Cars can be a death trap. I prefer the freedom of being able to make a run for it if I have to."

"What's the rush, Gabe? We're doing fine here; and I don't have a good feeling about you going out there by yourself. Let's enjoy one more peaceful day, and then I'll go with you, tomorrow." Eden found herself anxiously rubbing Gabe's arm. He glanced down at her hand, and she quickly removed it.

"Okay, I'll stick around until tomorrow," Gabe said. "But I don't want you going with me. You should stay here with Jane."

"Charlotte will look after her; and I'll feel better if you have some backup."

"Any particular reason why you don't think I'm capable of handling the task alone?"

"I know you're capable; it's just that I don't want you out there alone."

"Why not?" Gabe stared at Eden, awaiting her response.

Eden fidgeted. "I guess I'm sort of reminded of the last time I saw my mother alive. She'd been abused by my stepfather for many years, and was going to file a domestic abuse report against him. She was going to leave him, and she and I were going to move into our own place. My stepfather is an important man in Mexico—lots of connections. Long story short, my mother never made it home. She disappeared without a trace. And I became my stepfather's new punching bag for the next five years."

"Wow! What kind of man would put his hands on women and children?"

"He was a monster. He had no more of a heart than those biters out there. That's why I escaped across the border. It's sort of ironic. My greatest fear was that my stepfather would come after me, and I never dreamed I'd be up against something worse—a plague of living dead."

"No one is gonna hurt you, Eden. I'll put a bullet in your step-father's head if he ever shows up. And as far as the biters… nothing's gonna happen to you. I got your back."

After months of staying strong while working the onion fields, and after seeing people she knew become afflicted with the infection that turned humans into beasts, Eden felt herself over-come with emotion. She fell against Gabriel and broke down and cried. Her face pressed against his broad chest, Eden quietly sobbed. Gabe enfolded her in his arms and gently stroked her hair.

CHAPTER 17

It appeared to be business as usual at the Bradley M. Jones Law Firm. Phones rang, FedEx packages were delivered, the fax machines whirred, and various staff members congregated around the water cooler to catch up on workplace gossip.

Inside his private office, Bradley hurriedly prepared documents that would transfer the Sherman Mansion deed to Elson Chandler. Preparing the documents was the easy part; getting them signed by the appropriate city officials would require crafty planning coupled with extreme cunning.

Last night, utilizing his exemplary oratory skills, Bradley had convinced Elson that he could seal the Sherman Mansion deal for him if he'd allow him to take Tessa home. Elson agreed on the condition that Bradley would turn over the deed to the mansion tonight. If he failed, Tessa would be forcibly returned to The Lilac, never to exit again.

With his daughter safe from vampires and recuperating in the comfort of her own home, Bradley needed to spend every second of his time making sure that she remained out of harm's way. But he was scheduled to appear in court at nine in the morning, and shirking his legal obligation could result in hefty fines, threats of disbarment, and possible jail time. Getting locked up even for a short time would not bode well for Tessa.

At precisely eight-forty-five, he grabbed his briefcase and

grudgingly headed toward the door. The courthouse was only a block away from his law firm; he'd make it there in less than ten minutes. Defending his guilty, scum bucket client was a bothersome chore—a complete waste of time that could be better spent putting together a persuasive presentation for the city officials.

As he neared the elevator, he bumped into Amy Horsheck.

"Morning, Mr. Jones," Amy murmured, her eyes self-consciously downcast.

"Morning, Amy," he said in a gruff tone, indicating he wasn't in a chatty mood.

"Mr. Jones," Amy blurted when Bradley strode past her.

"What is it? I have to be in court in a few minutes," he said irritably.

"Are you all right?" Looking for signs of puncture wounds, her eyes scanned him quickly.

"I'm fine," he said tersely.

"Well, I was wondering…" she said, her voice lowered to a conspiratorial whisper. "Apparently, the local police are in cahoots with the vampires, and I wondered if you were planning to involve city officials in this crisis. I know you have connections, and—"

Bradley looked down at his watch. "If you'll excuse me, I'm late for court," he said, brushing her aside.

Amy clutched the sleeve of his jacket. "But…but…Mr. Jones, aren't you going to do something to stop those awful vampires? They expect Derek and me to routinely donate blood. It's cruel and unreasonable. Abiding by their rules has turned our lives into an endless hell. We can't continue living like this."

Bradley eased his sleeve from Amy's clenched fingers. "Have you considered relocating—during daytime hours?" Bradley said coolly. After the real estate deal was completed, he fully intended on getting him and his daughter far away from Frombleton. He didn't care what happened to his greedy ex-wife. It would serve

Nicole right if the vampires drank every ounce of her blood. Hmm. Perhaps, he'd make a recommendation to Elson to feed on Tessa's money-grubbing mother.

"The vampires have humans spying for them during the day; we'd never make it out of Frombleton," Amy hurriedly whispered as she struggled to keep pace with Bradley's brisk strides.

"Spies...during the day?" Bradley muttered.

Amy nodded.

He realized that Walsh and Canelli were conspiring with the vampires, but he hadn't considered that there might be other humans involved.

"The spies are high school kids that pal around with vampires. They've been going door-to-door, pretending to solicit funds for a children's hospital. Being the charitable person that I am, I opened the door and let those despicable teens into my home. And now my husband and I are blood slaves to vampires. There has to be a way out of this!"

My God! The vampires have high school kids working for them, too! He was grateful for the heads up. He'd planned on sending Tessa back to school after she was feeling better, but not now. Tessa definitely wouldn't be returning to Frombleton High or going anywhere else for that matter. From now on, his daughter would be home-schooled. To keep Tessa safe, he'd have an updated security system installed, and he'd warn Nicole not to open the door to any teens that were asking for donations.

Returning his attention to Amy, Bradley held out his hands in a gesture of helplessness. "I don't know what to tell you, Amy. For now, I suggest you continue to keep your weekly appointments with the vampires. Believe me, you wouldn't like the alternative." He reached the elevator bank and impatiently pressed the "down" button.

"The alternative must be pretty awful, huh? Derek and I... We heard the noises from down the hall. Piercing screams, crying, and terrible moaning. It sounded like people were being slaughtered." She eyed him curiously. "What goes on, down the hall, in the doom room?"

"Unspeakable horrors," Bradley answered, shaking his head as gruesome memories flashed in his mind. "You'll be okay as long as you do what you've agreed to do."

"But we were tricked into signing on as blood donors. Mr. Jones, you have to help us get out of our contract. You're a respected man here in Frombleton. Can't you speak to the mayor. Don't you think he should know what's happening in his city?"

"I intend to speak to him, uh, eventually, but it may take some time to convince the mayor that vampires are actually in our midst. For the time being, it would be wise for you and Derek to keep your appointments." Bradley gave Amy a sympathetic pat on the shoulder and then stepped inside the elevator.

⊕ ⊕ ⊕

After an outburst by the defendant's rowdy family, the judge dismissed the proceedings until the next morning. Getting an unexpected early dismissal allowed Bradley time to work on his presentation and to scrutinize the long-winded, awkwardly worded deed that had been notarized back in 1897.

With an estimated value of fifteen thousand dollars, the Sherman Mansion was sold by Tallulah Sherman on April 25, 1897 for one dollar. According to the deed, the property was released unto to Mayor Judd Purcell of said Frombleton, Georgia and to his successors that may be elected from time to time, according to the law.

It appeared that transferring the deed didn't require as many signatures as Bradley had thought. He only needed one: the mayor's.

Judd Purcell was long gone. For the past one hundred years, he'd been residing in the Rolling Lawn Cemetery, but the current mayor, Ashton Ringwood, was alive and kicking. Over the phone, Bradley spoke to the mayor about an amazing opportunity that would bring in millions of dollars of revenue to the city of Frombleton, and Bradley was granted a private meeting with Mayor Ringwood.

Relying on his gift of gab, Bradley arrived at City Hall around one in the afternoon and spent the next two hours trying to convince Ringwood that signing over the museum to an eccentric billionaire who had a penchant for the Sherman Mansion would get the bankrupt city of Frombleton out of debt.

"Why are you being such a stubborn cuss?" Bradley said with an anxious laugh.

"The deal sounds shaky. I can forget about getting reelected if I throw away a historical treasure on a bogus deal."

"But the mansion is costing the city more than it's bringing in. I've done my research, Ringwood, and the Sherwin Mansion is not bringing in enough to pay the monthly utilities. My guy will take it off the city's hands and with his proposal to bring in a soccer stadium and a casino, before you know it, Frombleton will be flourishing."

"Folks here aren't that interested in soccer," the mayor stated.

"They'll develop an interest. Give the town something to do in the summer months. The stadium can also be used for concerts and other events."

Ringwood scratched his head. "I don't know, Bradley. I need to meet this billionaire guy...uh, what's his name, again?"

"Chandler. Elson Chandler."

Ringwood scowled. "Doesn't ring a bell. Never heard of him."

"New money. He's involved in oil deals with the uh, Arabs."

"Yeah, well, I need to hear the proposal from this Chandler fellow, firsthand."

"Sure, okay." There was uncertainty in Bradley's voice.

"Hey, wanna hear something bizarre," Ringwood said, changing the subject. "We got a call this morning from a woman who claimed her kid was snatched—a two-year-old. She said she was afraid to reveal her identity for fear from retaliation."

Bradley leaned forward, his mouth suddenly dry. "Retaliation from whom?"

The mayor gestured with his hands. "Beats me. Aliens, vampires—something kooky like that. Every nutjob in the city thinks it's their prerogative to pick up the phone and make crazy complaints to the mayor." Shaking his head, he picked up the bottle and poured himself yet another drink, and took a generous swig.

Glancing nervously at his watch, a shiver of horror went through Bradley as he realized there were only a few hours left before the sun went down. The absurd idea that Tessa might possibly be snatched from her bed and be forced to endure another grisly ordeal was more than Bradley could bear. He'd scarcely withstood the prolonged, and multiple bites he'd received from those terrible vampires, and in her weakened condition, Tessa would not survive another attack.

His eyes darted to the window, and he was shocked to see the sun disappearing behind dark clouds. The sky was streaked with ominous shades of brown and gray. "The sky's darkening," he said in a quivering voice.

"Yeah, it's supposed to rain. That hot female meteorologist on channel six mentioned there'd be light showers."

His mind on the vampires, Bradley gave the mayor a blank look.

"You know the girl I'm talking about...long brown hair, big innocent eyes. She's always wearing short, sexy dresses that show off legs for days." Ringwood smiled lecherously. "I'd sure like to snuggle up on a rainy day with the weather girl."

As Ringwood fantasized about an illicit tryst with a TV personality, Bradley agonized over the possibility of Tessa being snatched from her bed. Examining the muddy brown sky through narrowed eyes, he wondered if the vampires would awaken earlier than usual or did they have an internal alarm clock that went off at the same time every night? The uncertainty caused his stomach to churn and his palms to sweat. *I shouldn't have gambled with Tessa's life; I should have fled the city last night*, he thought regretfully.

Mayor Ringwood opened a drawer and pulled out a bottle of Scotch and two shot glasses. "You're looking like you lost your best friend, fella. This'll cheer you up. It's twenty-five-year-old scotch. Good stuff!" the mayor boasted.

Bradley threw back the drink and slammed his glass on the mayor's desk. "Yeah, it's good stuff; give me another," he said, grateful for the opportunity to self-medicate.

"Only the best for the mayor of Frombleton," Mayor Ringwood said cheerfully as he refilled Bradley's glass and then poured himself another drink as well.

His mind racing against time, Bradley decided that his only option was to lure the mayor to The Lilac. Let Elson and his henchmen coerce Ringwood into signing.

In a brighter mood, Bradley offered Ringwood a cheery smile. "What's on your schedule tonight? I believe I can set something up with Mr. Chandler at around seven tonight."

"On one condition."

"What's that?"

"A wealthy man like this Chandler fellow should be able to have any chick he wants, right?"

Bradley gave an uncertain head nod.

"Tell him to get me a brunette from one of those exclusive escort services in Atlanta. Someone that looks like the weather girl." Ringwood winked his eye conspiratorially.

"I'm sure that's not a problem for Mr. Chandler," Bradley said.

"And tell him to send a limo for me. I don't want to draw any attention. You know, making side deals while riding around in a city vehicle."

"Sure; I understand. See you tonight." This time, Bradley winked.

CHAPTER 18

Not a man to throw around good money, Bradley M. Jones hated having to come out of pocket to pay for a limo ride for the mayor. But he supposed he should count his blessings. Arranging for a limo service was a lot easier than getting Elson on the phone. He was on hold for an eternity, all the while praying that Elson would not impulsively send his crew of deadly vampires after Tessa. Though he'd warned Nicole to lock the doors, arm the alarm system, and hide Tessa in the attic, he doubted if ordinary security measures would deter a determined and deranged vampire like Chaos. He knew for certain that Chaos could scale walls, and he was probably proficient at picking locks. There was no doubt that the fiend could sniff out Tessa's hiding place in a hot minute.

Yes, paying for the limo was a small price.

Giving the limo the thumbs-up sign, the mayor, reeking of alcohol, joined Bradley in the back. After examining the minibar, his mouth turned down. "What's with the economy-priced liquor. Your Arab guy gets a strike against him for stocking the bar with cheap alcohol."

"He's not an Arab; he's in business with them," Bradley said, sticking to the story he'd devised.

"Whatever." The mayor reached into his inside pocket and pulled out a flask. "I brought the good stuff with me. Good thing

I'm always prepared." The limo glided toward the highway, and Ringwood glanced out the tinted window. "Where's he staying—The Atwell Hotel or is he leasing a swanky place outside of town?"

"We're going downtown to meet him."

"Yeah, I can see that," Ringwood said, turning the flask up to his lips. He wiped his mouth with the back of his hand and began muttering angrily to himself.

"Are you okay?" Bradley asked.

"You can ask me that question after my rendezvous with the high-class hooker."

Bradley frowned in confusion.

"I asked for an escort from one of those pricey agencies," Ringwood clarified.

"Oh, right…right."

"The rich guy is taking care of that, isn't he?"

This moron has got to be kidding me! "Yes, I informed him that you were interested in a date that resembled the meteorologist on channel six, and his assistant is taking care of it—absolutely."

"I'm getting a boner just thinking about that weather-forecasting broad," Ringwood exclaimed and took another swig from his flask.

Jesus! What a creep! Dealing with Ringwood was like trying to placate a petulant child. Bradley and the mayor had been casual acquaintances for several years, and though he'd heard about the man's drinking problem, he'd never realized that Ringwood was such an extremely obnoxious individual.

Luckily, when the limo turned down the raunchy side street that led to the back entrance of The Lilac, Ringwood wasn't paying any attention. Deep in thought, his eyes were closed as he sipped aged scotch. His mind, no doubt, was occupied with forbidden fantasies of him and the weather girl.

The driver pulled up to the curb in front of The Lilac, and Ringwood's eyes popped open. Frowning at the abandoned hotel, he spat, "Hey! I'm not going in there; why'd you bring me to this rundown dump? Is this your idea of a practical joke?"

"No, Mr. Chandler is an eccentric man; he and his people prefer meeting in, uh, secluded settings." Bradley gazed out at the crumbling building, looking for a sign of activity.

"Secluded!" Ringwood scoffed. "That word doesn't begin to describe this decrepit place!"

Bradley made a helpless gesture. "The superrich can be odd birds, at times."

"I want you to turn this limo around, and tell those *Shahs of Sunset* to arrange a meeting in a decent hotel—something that hasn't been shut down for a quarter of a century." Ringwood sat back. Refusing to budge, he stubbornly crossed his arms over his chest.

The driver suddenly opened the back door and without warning, he yanked Bradley out by the collar.

The mayor let out a surprised yelp. "What the hell is going on? Get your filthy hands off me! I'm the mayor of Frombleton; you can't treat me like this. I'm going to report your behavior to your employer, and I guarantee you, you can kiss your job goodbye."

"Is that so?" the bullishly strong driver said in a voice filled with menace. At that moment, Bradley realized the driver was a vampire. It shouldn't have surprised him that the long arm of Elson Chandler had reached the limousine service.

The vampire-driver slashed Ringwood across the face with a sharpened fingernail and then flung him to the ground with brutal force. The back door of the hotel creaked open, and three grinning, pallid-faced vampires immediately swooped down on the mayor. Ringwood howled with rage, hurling profanities as he tried to fight off the vampires.

Overpowering the mayor, two vampires bit into his flesh, while the third—a woman—kicked Ringwood in the side repeatedly. She hissed and emitted low growls with each kick, her eyes flaring with irrational hostility.

Recognizing the hateful woman as the lullaby-singer that had murdered the little boy last night, Bradley shrank back in fear, afraid that meeting her eye might trigger irrational violence directed at him.

After five or so minutes, the growling, kicking, and noisy blood-guzzling ceased. Moaning miserably, Ringwood was dragged down a dusty hallway by the female vampire. The two males followed behind. Moving at a leisurely pace, they swiped blood spatters from their clothing, and made awful slurping sounds as they lapped crimson blood from their palms up to their fingertips.

Tagging along sheepishly, Bradley was halted by the limo driver. "You stay here," the driver said firmly. Looking around the dim environment, Bradley decided that the cobwebbed area appeared to have once been the hotel lobby.

He paced anxiously for a good ten minutes. Hopefully, the mayor hadn't been so badly maimed and traumatized that he was unable to sign his name to the documents that were still inside Bradley's briefcase.

With any luck, the vampires had taken Ringwood to Elson. Elson would keep the mayor alive long enough to sign the paperwork. Although Elson had his moments of savagery, he behaved in a civilized manner most of the time. In fact, Elson and the girl named Ismene seemed to be the only sane vampires in the pack. Chaos, the female vocalist, and all the others were deranged, bloodthirsty lunatics!

Worried sick that vampires like Chaos and the crazy vampire woman would lapse into a blood-crazed frenzy before Ringwood could sign the papers, Bradley began pacing again. If the vampires killed Ringwood, Tessa's life would be in jeopardy. Bradley's breath quickened, and a pulse pounded at his temple as he worried about his daughter's safety.

Physically fatigued and emotionally spent, he finally stopped pacing and set his briefcase on the floor. He collapsed into a dust-covered chair. With his hands folded on his lap, he gazed at the flame of the lone candle that burned on top of an outdated concierge desk. The flickering flame had a calming effect, and he closed his eyes as he waited to learn Tessa's fate. It was out of his hands now; there was nothing more he could do. If Elson decided to go after Tessa, Bradley's final option would be to steal the limo, speed to his ex-wife's house and do the job himself. A swift death would be an act of kindness when compared to being tortured endlessly by a pack of bloodsucking, soulless vampires.

But how could he kill Tessa and Nicole swiftly when his gun was locked in a safe in his condo? He pondered for a few seconds, and decided that a knife through their hearts would be quick and efficient. But what about him—in what manner would he end his own miserable life? He couldn't very well stab himself to death. After brief contemplation, he came to the conclusion that hanging himself was his only option. No! That wouldn't work. He didn't have any experience with tying a sturdy and effective noose, and the process seemed time-consuming and complex. He could undoubtedly find the directions online, but that would give the vampires time to find and apprehend him. Slashing his wrists was the quickest way out, Bradley concluded.

He became melancholy as he thought about how much of Tessa's life he had missed while climbing the ladder of success. He'd been absent at too many birthday parties, too many school events. Now, all his achievements seemed petty and meaningless;

he'd give anything for the opportunity to be a good father. His eyes glimmered with tears. Tessa was an innocent child; she didn't deserve to lose her life so soon and so violently. Even gold-digging Nicole didn't deserve such a brutal ending.

Imagining the headlines in *The Frombleton Daily News*, Bradley smiled wryly. *Topnotch criminal defense attorney commits savage double homicide and then slashes his wrists.* The media would have a field day with this one.

Sighing, he scanned the old lobby, and looking downward, he noticed that the faded letters in the center of the tattered carpet spelled out, "The Lilac" in fanciful script. The old hotel had seen better days. He closed his eyes and considered praying, but decided that even God himself couldn't help him now.

In his mind, he pictured Tessa in happier times. He pictured her listening to music through headphones while singing loudly and off-key. He recalled their most recent argument, which seemed rather silly now. Tessa wanted a new car for her upcoming sixteenth birthday, but Bradley had resisted, believing his daughter to be too immature to take on the responsibility of owning and operating a car.

He smiled to himself, recalling how Tessa had persistently shown him images of shiny sports cars. His daughter had always been able to wrap him around her finger. *When this nightmare is over, you're getting your car, sweetheart,* he vowed. *Any car you want will be delivered with a big, red ribbon wrapped around it…and you won't have to wait until your birthday to get it.*

Suddenly sensing movement, Bradley jumped in alarm and rose to his feet. He jerked his head back and forth, but with the dim lighting of the candle, he only caught a glimpse of something moving quickly.

He heard a rustling sound and saw a dark blur in the corner of his eye. Panic flared within him. Could it be a rat? God, he hated rodents. His face contorted, and his eyes swept the floor. The next sound he heard was the soft peel of laughter...or was someone crying? Something shot past him, and Bradley whirled around, eyes wide open, as he tried to make out the indistinguishable forms in the gloomy lobby.

"Hello? Is anyone there?" he called in a hushed, quavering voice. Turning in a full circle, he shouted in a frightened, high octave, "Who's there!" No response. Although the lobby was eerily still and quiet, he sensed a presence. Felt as if he was being watched.

Propelled by fear, he grabbed the candle and began searching the lobby. The flickering flame cast eerie shadows. The silhouette of a lamp shade resembled a large and sinister hat, and Bradley flinched in fear and reeled backward.

With an inexplicable knowing, Bradley realized with a jolt that something was hiding behind the concierge desk. He picked up his briefcase and using it as a shield, he clutched it in front of him as he crept toward the desk. A quick peek revealed nothing, but as he waved the candle around, he saw something that caused him to blink in astonishment.

Crouched in a corner behind the desk was a child—a leering little boy with ghastly pale skin and sporting a glistening pair of deadly fangs. Recognizing the child's blood-encrusted Old Navy T-shirt, Bradley's throat went dry as he backed away unsteadily.

Before Bradley could process the ungodly sight, he heard a familiar, croaking voice. "Babeeeee! Where's my beautiful little baby?" sang a familiar, scratchy voice.

Oh, dear God—not her! Bradley pointed the candle in the direction of the entrance, wondering if he should risk trying to outrun the crazed vampire singer. Surely, he could make a clean getaway if he hopped in the limo and locked all the doors. He frowned, remembering the unnatural strength and agility of vampires. The psychotic singer was liable to burst through the limo's windshield or rip one of the doors from the hinges.

Shakily holding the candle and hoping that the flame might protect him from an attack, Bradley trudged over to the dusty chair and slumped in the seat.

"Baby! Stop fooling around; Mommy has no patience for childishness!" called the vampire in a voice charged with anger.

Mommy? Astonished, Bradley mouth gaped open. The vicious, deranged vampire woman had transformed an innocent child into one of the living dead!

Responding to the stern tone, the child toddled out from behind the desk.

"Come to Mommy; I have something for you," the vampire woman said, softening her ornery tone. She held up a baby's bottle that was filled with a dark red liquid that was undoubtedly blood.

The patter of tiny footsteps sounded as the child rushed toward its new guardian. Reaching urgently for the bottle of blood, the boy hissed and whimpered in his eagerness to feed. Lips locked onto the nipple, he sucked greedily for several moments, and then began crying in frustration when the blood didn't flow quickly enough. Using his strong, sharpened teeth, the boy ripped the rubber nipple in half. With his head thrown back, he guzzled blood, draining the bottle in a few seconds flat. Then he shook the empty bottle, and glared at it in rage and disbelief. Wailing angrily, he hurled the bottle across the room. At the calamitous sound of glass shattering against the wall, the boy's teary eyes lit with satisfaction for a few fleeting moments.

"Bad boy; you're a bad, bad boy. That's the only bottle left;

now you'll have to feed like Mommy and the other grownups."
She shook her head in disappointment and then lifted the child
into her arms.

Sniffing the air, the boy set his gaze on Bradley. Worked into a
frenzy, the child squirmed and squealed, and relentlessly attempted
to launch himself toward the scent of fresh blood.

"No, you can't drink his blood; Elson says the lawyer is off
limits." She cast a hateful gaze Bradley's way, as if Bradley were
responsible for Elson's decision. The boy fought and squealed,
struggling to leap out of his guardian's arms. Teeth gnashing, he
snapped at the air as he tried to get at Bradley. Turning on his
guardian, the ferocious boy's teeth locked onto the sleeve of her
dress. She yanked the fabric from his clenched teeth. "Calm
down, calm down; there's lots of fresh blood upstairs," she said
in a cajoling tone. Holding the boy firmly, she turned around
and departed the lobby through an oval entryway.

The woman and child vanished in the darkness and Bradley
was flooded with relief. He grasped the handle of his briefcase,
fondling the leather strap reassuringly. The documents enclosed
were his only ticket out of the petrifying, nightmare world that
held him captive.

CHAPTER 19

The candle's flame grew dimmer and he estimated the weakening glow would last no more than five minutes, tops. *What's taking them so long?* Bradley wondered, craning his neck toward the entryway, hoping to see the bulky figure of the limo driver or perhaps Elson, himself. Bradley had completed his end of the bargain—he'd delivered the mayor and had drawn the paperwork. It wasn't his fault that the mayor's signature had yet to be secured.

It would be fantastic if he and Elson could shake on it and conclude the unpleasant business venture. But it didn't seem likely that Elson would let him walk away with no strings attached. Bradley glanced at the fading candle flame again, and resigned himself to sitting and waiting in pitch darkness.

"Good evening, counselor." A feminine voice that held a hint of amusement, drifted through the darkness and seemed to tickle his ear.

"Uh, good evening," Bradley replied, squinting and straining to make out the face that belonged to the voice.

"It's Ismene. Elson's ready to see you. Come with me." She grasped his hand lightly, and he inwardly cringed at her ice-cold touch.

"Excuse the coldness of my hand; it's been so busy here tonight, I haven't had time to feed," she said in a polite tone. Bradley nodded and smiled uncomfortably.

She guided him out of the lobby and down an unlit corridor that was so dark, he might as well have been wearing a blindfold. Ismene walked swiftly, and though she held his hand, he used the other to grope and feel his way through the darkness.

They climbed many flights of dark and forbidding stairs, and in the distance he could hear a chorus of howls that no doubt came from a new group of humans who had foolishly risked their lives by refusing to give blood willingly. Bradley's heart went out to the victims that were being confined in the doom room. Before the night was over, they'd all end up mutilated, blood-drained, or turned into one of the undead. He shuddered at the thought of the toddler vampire. That poor kid would spend the rest of eternity drinking blood from a baby's bottle or perhaps he'd advance to a Sippy cup. He'd never again feel sunlight on his face; he'd never learn to ride a bike, or play soccer. Hell, he'd never mature enough to even learn his ABC's.

By the time they reached the fifth floor, Bradley was winded and perspiring. Ismene, on the other hand, made the hike up the numerous flights of stairs without any signs of distress. The hall-way was illuminated with glowing candles that highlighted what appeared to be ancient artwork, mounted on walls that were painted in hues of brown, bronze, and gold—masculine colors that symbolized power. This, undoubtedly, was Elson Chandler's floor.

Ismene rapped sharply on a mahogany door, opened it, and gestured for Bradley to enter. With exotic animal-fur wall hangings, tribal masks, and a collection of woodcarvings, Elson's suite reminded Bradley of Africa. Set on a polished wood table was what appeared to be a solid gold chess set. Engaged in a chess match, Elson and Chaos sat across from each other, silently studying the gleaming pieces.

Bradley had never seen Chaos sitting still. Having previously exhibited the traits of an ADHD adult, Chaos had seemed incapable of quiet contemplation. It was a relief to be in his presence without having to duck and dodge as the energetic vampire took flying leaps and engaged in wild performances that caused walls to shake.

Collapsed on an antique sofa, Mayor Ringwood was beat up and bloody with claw marks on his face, a deep gash on the top of his head, and numerous puncture wounds covering his neck. Though Bradley felt a stab of pity for the man, he was also relieved that this time it was the mayor, and not he, who had ignited the wrath of the vampires.

"Our friend is ready to sign the paperwork, isn't that right?" Elson said to Ringwood.

"If you say so, but you might as well have a gun to my head," Ringwood slurred, and it was hard to tell if his speech had been affected by too much liquor or severe blood loss.

"Whether or not you sign is completely up to you," Elson said coldly, cutting an eye at Chaos. Chaos pushed his chair back fiercely. Leaning forward and leering in anticipation, Chaos didn't require much goading; he seemed eager to pounce on the mayor.

Ringwood's arm went up defensively. "Keep that madman away from me! Geez, I'm gonna need a transfusion if you guys don't let up with the constant biting. I'm getting nauseous."

"Are you ready to sign the property over to me?" Elson said, taking steps toward Ringwood.

"I guess, but, um…I have to say something on behalf of my constituents that you're holding hostage downstairs. What you're forcing them to do is inhumane and opposes everything this great country stands for." He dropped his eyes in shame. "People have been warning me. They've been calling my office complaining about vampires swarming our fine city, but I didn't listen. I thought they were all batshit crazy." Ringwood groaned miserably. "I failed them. A good mayor should always listen to the voice of the people."

Elson applauded. "Great speech, Mr. Mayor, but you should save it for your next campaign. I'm sure the people will rally behind a man that promises to rid the city of evil vampires."

Ringwood's face twisted in bafflement. "What are you saying?"

"Don't be too hard on yourself, fellow. I'm going to put my power behind you, and you're going to get through this smelling like a rose. Let's get together in a week or so, after I've settled in at the mansion. We'll have dinner and discuss our future in politics. With you running the city as merely a figurehead, we'll be able to accomplish great things together."

"A figurehead—what are you saying?"

"I'm saying that from now on, you'll be mayor in name only; I'll be the one who's really running this town."

"Oh, I see," Ringwood said, looking sickened.

"Glad we see eye to eye." Elson gave Ringwood a slap on the back.

"Ow, go easy. Every part of my body hurts." Wincing, Ringwood ran a finger over the punctures on his neck. "You didn't have to sic those vampires on me to get your point across. I was lured here under false pretenses. Your friend here…" Frowning in repugnance, he nodded toward Bradley. "He told me you're in business with Arabs and that you're filthy rich from big oil deals. Is there any truth to the story that you're interested in opening a few casinos and spreading some of your wealth around Frombleton?"

"Bradley has a vivid imagination. Though I'm quite wealthy, I didn't get my fortune from oil, nor do I plan on venturing into the casino industry. But don't worry, Mr. Mayor, I have a few ideas to increase the revenue of Frombleton. We'll get together soon. Now, stop stalling and sign the papers."

"Sure. No problem."

Elson gave Bradley a head nod and Bradley opened his brief-case. He retrieved the folder that contained the important documents, and then spread them out on an elegant, wood-carved coffee table. "Sign here...here...and here, Mr. Mayor," Bradley said, pointing eagerly at each page that required a signature.

As Ringwood hastily scrawled his name, Bradley noticed twin, gaping holes in his wrist. As despicable a character as the mayor was, he couldn't help feeling a little sorry for the guy. He'd lost a lot tonight: blood, his distinguished position, and his dignity.

Ringwood signed the last page and then struggled to his feet. "That's that," he said as he attempted to smooth out his torn and crinkled suit. "If you don't mind, I'd like to call myself a cab. There's no way I'm getting back in the limo with that bloodthirsty driver."

"You're forgetting something," Ismene said, stepping forward.

"What's that?"

"You don't make decisions anymore, Elson does." She glanced at Elson. "Any preference on how the mayor gets home?"

"He can take a cab, but make sure the cabbie gives a pint of blood and is added to the donors list."

"I'll take care of it," Ismene responded.

CHAPTER 20

He was tired. His limbs felt leaden—too heavy to function properly. Moving lethargically, Walter Sutton was unable to keep up with the pack. While the other flesh-eaters swiftly followed the scent of blood, Walter slowly dragged what was left of his decaying body, emitting grunts and garbled cries of frustration. By the time he reached the human prey, the pack had already fed and had moved on, leaving nothing for Walter except a ragged carcass. No juicy innards, no bloody clumps of meat. There was nothing except shredded clothing, clusters of hair, and bare bones.

He hovered over the carcass and broke off a skeletal finger. Chomping into the bone, he frantically sucked out the marrow. Dissatisfied and violently hunger, he flung the bony finger and growled in rage. Grabbing tufts of hair from the pavement, he hungrily nibbled on the bits of scalp that were attached to the patches of hair. But the painful hunger continued, cutting through him like a fiery knife.

His former identity, Walter Sutton, onion farmer, was no longer a part of his memory. In fact, he had no memory at all. No recollection of relatives or friends or any aspect of his human existence. It had been weeks since he'd last fed, but Walter had no concept of time. His level of awareness completely revolved around his ravenous desire to consume flesh and blood.

Alerted by movement and the scent of warm blood, he reached out a rotting hand toward a speeding car that was swerving dangerously out of control as it traveled along the deserted road. Due to an injury, or maybe from sheer panic alone, the driver lost control and slammed into a telephone pole. The loud boom announced the collision, and somewhere in Walter's consciousness was the knowledge that injured prey was near.

For flesh-eaters, the explosion of sound had the same effect as the ring of a dinner bell. Acting more out of impulse than hunger, the pack of living dead that had fed only a few minutes ago, turned around and began flocking toward the crash site. Ambling as swiftly as their uncoordinated bodies would allow, they grunted and drooled with excitement.

In his haste to join in the feeding frenzy, Walter's legs gave out, and he fell to the ground. Lying on his stomach, he was unable to gather enough strength to push himself up from the pavement and rise to his feet. Relying on pure instinct, he used blackened fingernails to dig into the concrete grooves and to slowly and determinedly pull himself along, but when it became too much of an effort to keep going, Walter groaned in misery and writhed on the ground. Driven mad by the scent of human blood, he cried out in pain and rage.

⊕ ⊕ ⊕

Jonas carried a shopping bag filled with fresh slabs of beef, packaged in brown paper and taped closed. As he slipped into the back of the mill, he could hear the rattling chains that secured the creatures that were known in their human lives as Pedro and Julia. Sensing Jonas was near, their chains clanked together vigorously, and their incomprehensible utterances grew louder and more fervent. The creatures had come to associate Jonas's presence with the procurement of food.

Usually, he'd take them into the woods and let them hunt or he'd bring them live poultry, but tonight he planned something else. Holland's spell had changed his way of eating and it would be a breakthrough if he was successful in changing the creatures' diets from living flesh to raw meat.

Inside the mill, he pulled out a package that was damp with blood. Enticed by the smell, his two charges became wild and cried out frantically as they attempted to break free of the chains that bound them. Jonas threw two bloody pieces of meat to the floor and Pedro quickly dropped down and snatched both pieces and stuffed them into his mouth. Left with nothing, Julia snarled in displeasure.

"Don't worry; I have something for you, too," Jonas said. He retrieved more raw meat, and threw the next two pieces in separate directions, aiming one slab near Julia and flinging the other Pedro's way. They devoured the beef and immediately began whining for more.

It worked! These creatures are evolving along with me. This could also be a solution for the other creatures that were prowling the streets in search of living food—a solution that would save human lives.

He smiled to himself as he evenly distributed the meat between Pedro and Julia. The pair had insatiable appetites and could have gorged without cessation if he allowed them to. After they'd eaten the last slab of beef, Jonas was certain they'd had more than enough to appease their immediate hunger. With a sense of satisfaction, he exited the mill.

After only a few paces, the inner peace and sense of well-being vanished. The roaring cries inside his head reminded him that he had to find the others. One cry rose above the others, and the connection was so powerful, it seemed to be yelling directly into his ears. The link between Jonas and whatever was pleading for help was so strong, he clutched his stomach as he experienced a visceral sensation of agonizing hunger. How could that be? He'd eaten only an hour ago. Dinner had been delivered to his hotel room—rare steak. Why was he feeling that cursed hunger again?

Who are you? Where are you—and why do I feel such a close connection to you? He closed his eyes and waited, as if expecting the answers to be whispered in his ear. But no answers came. Instead, the cry grew faint and muffled in his head, and finally there was silence. A strong, sudden impulse seemed to pull Jonas northward.

Hands jammed in his pockets, Jonas walked briskly, following his impulses. Possessing great speed, Jonas found he'd traveled about thirty miles. As he crossed into Willow Hills, he noticed the town was quiet. It appeared deserted with cars piled up on the roads, but no drivers behind the wheels. Where was everyone? Had the whole town fled for their lives or had they all been transformed into cursed, flesh-eaters? He felt a sick sensation as he moved onward, peeking in the windows of uninhabited houses and abandoned businesses.

A pitiful sound caught his attention, and he whirled to the right, spotting a lone figure sprawled out on the concrete about fifty yards ahead. Jonas galloped forward, bracing himself for the stench and the jolting visual of the decomposing body of another poor soul. When he reached the wretched creature, it was lying on its belly, crying and writhing, but was too weak to turn itself over.

Flooded with sympathy, Jonas got down on one knee. "I'll help you," he said, turning the thing onto its back. Though decomposition had eaten away at its face, and there were only holes where its ears used to be, Jonas saw a glimmer of familiarity and then, gasped in recognition. *I know you; I've seen you before.* He stared at what was left of the face, and vague memories flashed across his mind. Pensively, his hand went to the center of his chest, and through the fabric of his shirt, Jonas could feel the scarred flesh that was caused by a bullet wound. And then he remembered.

It's him! It's the onion farmer that kidnapped me from the boat. The man that shot and buried me alive. Jonas shuddered as memories flooded his mind. He relived the shocking pain of having a bullet tearing into his flesh, and he vividly recalled the terrible fear he'd experienced when piles of dirt were shoveled over his paralyzed body.

But instead of anger or hatred; he felt only pity for the monster he'd created. *So, this is how it all began. I bit the farmer, and somehow created a ravenous brood of flesh-eaters.*

Jonas pulled the farmer to his feet, but he wobbled and then toppled back down. Realizing that the farmer didn't have the strength to stand on his, Jonas lifted him and tossed him over a shoulder. A block away was the shopping district with an assortment of restaurants and grocery stores. Effortlessly, Jonas carried the farmer, taking him to the first restaurant he encountered. Inside the abandoned bistro, he gingerly placed the farmer's rotting body on the floor. "Hang on," he told the groaning farmer, and then made his way to the walk-in refrigerator in the rear. Jonas examined the contents in the refrigerator and began filling an oversized, metal mixing bowl with raw chicken, ground beef, and pork.

The farmer smelled the raw meat and went wild, struggling to get to his feet. Jonas knelt down and fed him handfuls of ground beef. And like the pair that was locked in the sugar mill, the farmer couldn't get enough. He kept opening his mouth for more, Jonas fed him until the metal bowl was empty. With his hunger satisfied, the farmer regained enough strength to stand and take slow steps, with Jonas's assistance.

"You've lost your ability to communicate, but on some level, I know you understand me," Jonas said, looking into the farmer's dull eyes. "I have to find the others—the creatures that are roaming around searching for living food. I have to help them, but I need you to stay here until I return."

Without a sound of complaint, the farmer allowed Jonas to guide him to the back of the empty restaurant and into a storage room with a desk and an office chair. Jonas nudged the farmer into the chair. Docile and compliant, he sat and stared into space. Jonas left the room and closed the fortified door, sliding the outside bolt into place.

CHAPTER 21

Not a single biter had been spotted all day, and Gabe convinced Leroy to make the trip with him to the Texaco station. Tony elected to stay behind and protect the women. Leroy furtively slid a gun to Eden. "This is my back-up weapon, and we're depending on you—not Tony—to hold things down until we get back," Leroy whispered.

"Thanks, Leroy. I appreciate it." She slipped the weapon in the back of her jeans, covering the handle with the oversized shirt Gabe had loaned her.

Gabe gave Eden a quick hug. She returned the gesture with an extra tight squeeze. "Hurry back," she murmured.

"It shouldn't take us more than thirty or forty minutes. Hopefully it's as quiet on Pelham Avenue as it's been around here."

Gabe and Leroy each carried a gas container, and headed out, on foot. Eden stood at the window watching them until they disappeared around the corner. Tony joined her at the window, gripping the nail gun. "How long did they say they'd be gone?" he asked in his typically shaky voice.

"About a half-hour."

"What exactly is the plan if the crazies show up? Am I supposed to run outside and start firing nails at 'em?" Sweat beads formed on his forehead, and his hands trembled slightly.

"Looks pretty peaceful out there, so why don't you put that

nail gun down?" She gave him a strained smile. "Why don't you go upstairs and check out the news—find out if CNN is reporting anything about the biters. I'll keep watch until the guys get back."

"Good idea." Tony set the nail gun down. "Give me a holler if you see anything out there."

"Sure," Eden said, relived when Tony wandered away. Having him hovering over her with a nail gun made her jumpy. Alone with her thoughts, she wondered what was happening with her and Gabe. Was it her imagination or had their friendship changed into something more intimate? Since she'd divulged her secrets about her stepfather, it seemed they'd established a different kind of closeness. Something tender and meaningful was beginning to develop between them. Like this morning, when she'd mentioned that she could use a change of clothes, Gabe had offered her one of the shirts that was packed in his duffle bag.

And when Gabe had hugged her before leaving with Leroy, it had taken all of her willpower not to lift her head and kiss him. She sensed he'd wanted to kiss her, too.

Smiling wistfully, she caressed Gabe's shirt. Bringing the collar up to her nose, she inhaled his masculine scent.

"Get out of here, weirdo!" Charlotte suddenly shouted. The high volume and irritation in her voice broke into Eden's pleasant thoughts. She hustled toward the storage room, and burst through the double doors. Surprisingly, Tony was in Charlotte's designated quarters, sitting on the cot. "I said, get out of here." Holding Jane, Charlotte stood over Tony, bristling with anger.

"What're you doing back here?" Eden asked Tony.

"I wanted to see the baby."

"He didn't even knock; just burst in here, and demanded to hold Jane," Charlotte said, scowling.

"What's wrong with that? I love kids. Don't have any of my

own, but I'm crazy about that sweet little angel." Tony stood and took steps toward Charlotte.

Eden blocked his path. "Are you all right, Tony? You don't look well," she said, noticing that he was twitching and perspiring badly.

"Yeah, I'm fine. Just wanna bounce that little cutie on my knee. She's got that sweet, baby smell. Makes me wanna bite those chubby cheeks." Eyes darting wildly, his mouth twisted into an obscene smile, and bits of saliva appeared in the corners of his mouth.

"You're not touching her; you creep!" Charlotte exploded. She shot a look at Eden. "He's acting strange; what do you think is wrong with him?"

Eden studied Tony suspiciously. "You don't look well, Tony. Why don't you go upstairs and lie down," Eden urged in a gentle tone.

"I don't wanna go upstairs. I'm tired of everyone telling me what to do!" He gestured with a sweeping motion that raised his shirt, and Eden winced when she spotted a deep scratch near his waistline.

She pointed to the angry abrasion. "What happened there?"

"It's nothing. I got scraped up by a bush while I was running from the crazies." Tony tugged on his shirt and covered the injury.

"That scrape looks infected; can I have a look at it?" Eden said with a hint of apprehension in her voice. The change in Tony's disposition reminded her of little Trey at the shelter. The child had gone from a quiet, agreeable little boy to a snarling and biting hellion. Trey had a scratch on his body also.

"Get out of my room; I need some privacy!" Tony bellowed irrationally.

"This isn't your room; Leroy has been letting Charlotte stay in here." Eden motioned for Charlotte to leave the room with Jane. Charlotte turned to leave, and Tony bolted after her.

"Bring that baby back! I'm not gonna bite her. I promise; I just wanna hold her!" Tony's fingers wiggled in eagerness. He licked at his lips as a yellowish drool poured from his mouth and ran down his chin.

Charlotte ran screaming with Jane and Eden drew the gun. "Back up, Tony. Back up or I'll shoot."

From outside the storage room, Jane began to wail. Unconcerned that a gun was pointed at him, Tony stormed toward the double door—growling, his jaws working up and down.

Holding the gun with both hands, Eden aimed at Tony's head, and pulled the trigger.

CHAPTER 22

arrett met the moving van at the gate of the Sherwood Mansion, and motioned for the driver to take the delivery to the service entrance. The van rumbled past the open gate, and twenty-two caskets were unloaded and lined side-by-side in the bowels of the cellar. Two caskets remained in the van: Elson's solid bronze casket and next to it was Ismene's. Ismene's coffin was white with the hand-painted images of red poppy and white chamomile flowers with a blue sky and sunshine background.

"These two go upstairs," Jarrett said and then pointed to the bronze casket. "Take that one to the master suite—east-wing. And be very, very careful." The four movers didn't ask any questions. They quietly and almost reverently removed the bronze casket from the van, their solemn faces suggesting that they probably thought the Sherman Mansion was now operating as a mortuary.

Alone with Ismene's coffin, Jarrett caressed the painted image that showed homage to the sunny sky that was lost to Ismene, forever.

Desiring privacy, he closed the van's door and was instantly engulfed in darkness. It was so dark, he considered lifting the lid of the coffin to steal a glance of his beautiful vampire girlfriend. No, he didn't dare; it was too risky. He'd never forgive himself if through a chink or a crack of some sort, a sliver of sunlight found its way inside the van. The sun that Ismene had immortalized on her private resting place could scorch her skin—it could destroy her. If something happened to Ismene, not only would Jarrett be unable to forgive himself...Elson wouldn't forgive him, either. And no matter how helpful Jarrett had become to the vampires, Elson would deliver a cruel death if he irresponsibly caused Ismene's demise.

He felt his heart begin to race at the very thought of losing Ismene. As badly as he wanted to gaze at his beloved, he realized that the consequences were not worth the risk.

When the movers returned, Jarrett instructed them to place Ismene's coffin in the small suite on the west wing. He checked the time and realized another van was scheduled to arrive soon. Jarrett scratched his head, wondering if the delivery would be the shipment of refrigerated blood or was the furniture and artwork scheduled next?

A truck bumped along the driveway and Jarrett was stunned to see the town's librarian, Tanya Fluegfelder, seated next to the driver. She slid down her window. "Hi there, Jarrett. I'm over-seeing Mr. Chandler's library, making sure that it's properly categorized."

"No one told me about this."

"Travis put me in charge. I believe he got permission from Mr. Chandler."

"Oh." Jarrett scanned the instructions on his clipboard, but there was nothing mentioned about Ms. Fluegfelder. He'd be facing a serious reprimand if he allowed someone in the mansion that didn't have any business being there. "How about I relieve you of those book shelves and boxes of books? I'll make sure they get where they're supposed to go," Jarrett said.

"But some of these books are rare and..." She paused, eyes shifting with fear and anxiety.

Jarrett could understand her anxiousness. Disobeying a vampire's instructions could have deadly consequences, but he had to think about numero uno. Tanya Fluegfelder was a sweet lady and easy on the eyes, but he wasn't willing to allow her pretty face to get him in trouble. "Listen, until I speak to Travis personally, I can't let you in the mansion. I'm sorry, Ms. Fluegfelder."

"That's fine. I understand," she said in her silvery, sweet voice. "Travis must have forgotten to mention that I'm the in-house librarian."

"Seems like he did, but I'll get it straightened out tonight."

Tanya nodded. It wasn't easy to deny such a good-looking woman entry, but he had to take every precaution while the vampires were sleeping. As far as he knew, Ms. Fluegfelder was merely a blood donor; he had no information that listed her as the official in-house librarian.

After the shelves and boxes of books were unloaded, Jarrett waved at the truck driver and Ms. Fluegfelder as they turned around and departed the premises. He sure hoped he wasn't in trouble for turning the librarian away. But for now, he'd rather be safe than sorry.

Handling the daytime segment of the move was too much responsibility and too much pressure for one person. Sophia and Jarrett were supposed to share the responsibility, but Sophia hadn't shown up. Knowing Sophia, she'd partied with Chaos until dawn and was probably at home, curled up in bed, while Jarrett had been busy, busting his butt since eight this morning. He intended to speak to Ismene and voice a complaint about Sophia's work ethic—perhaps he'd suggest some type of painful punishment.

What would be a suitable punishment for Sophia? Jarrett wondered. The average person would loathe getting bitten by a gang of vampires, but Sophia was so masochistic, she loved it. No point in suggesting any kind of vampire retaliation. The best way to get even with Sophia was to ban her from vampire activities for a few weeks. He could feel a sneaky smile curving the corner of his lips as he pictured Sophia's response to discovering she was no longer welcome at vampire parties.

⊕ ⊕ ⊕

The party being held in the parlor was in celebration of Elson's first day in the mansion, and Jarrett had attended the gathering dressed in his best suit. There were perhaps a dozen of Elson's favorite offspring in attendance, as well as Mayor Ringwood and a couple of his City Hall cronies. Jarrett also noticed Tanya Fluegfelder was among the guests. The petite librarian's arm was linked with Travis's beefy arm. *When did they become a couple?* He supposed she'd been telling the truth about her position at the mansion. Travis was coarse and gruff, while Ms. Fluegfelder was a soft-spoken, delicate flower. They made an odd pairing and Jarrett wondered what they had in common. Glancing around, he noticed that Chaos was there with Sophia and several other human pets.

Mayor Ringwood was all smiles as he socialized with the vampire crowd, but Jarrett could tell that he was nervous by the subtle quivering of his bottom lip and the droplets of perspiration that gleamed on his face.

Ismene had been busy for most of the evening, assisting Elson and making sure the blood donor rooms were operating in an organized manner. The new doom room was housed in the basement. Actually, the space that was reserved for human rebels was located in an area of the basement that resembled an old-fashioned dungeon. The basement must have been soundproof because Jarrett didn't hear the usual chorus of terrified screams and pained groans that used to emanate when they were at The Lilac.

He watched Ms. Fluegfelder and Travis crossing the room, coming toward him. *I hope I'm not in trouble.*

"How ya doing tonight, Jarrett?" Travis said in his strong, Southern twang. "I hear there was a mix-up this afternoon between you and my sweetie." Clearly smitten, Travis looked upon the librarian with a warm smile, and then turned a surly gaze on Jarrett.

"Yeah, my bad. No one told me she was supposed to be working in the mansion during the day."

"Now you know," Travis said gruffly. "Tanya has fantastic organizational skills. The next time I hear about you interfering with her work, you're gonna find yourself looking a lot paler and weighing a whole lot less. Catch my drift?"

"Yeah, man. I said I'm sorry."

Travis wrapped his arm around Tanya's shoulder. "Let's go mingle, sweetheart."

"Sure," Tanya said, casting Jarrett an apologetic look.

It appeared that pretty much everyone at the gathering was hooked up with somebody. Everyone was happily in love, except Jarrett. Ismene was stuck to Elson like glue. If Jarrett didn't know better, he'd think they were lovers. Feeling unloved and neglected, he guzzled down a glass of red wine. Its dry and bitter taste suited his mood perfectly.

When Ismene finally joined him, Jarrett was feeling a little tipsy and argumentative. He complained that Sophia had been a no-show this morning. "I think she should be banished from future vampire events."

"Elson doesn't get involved in disciplining Chaos's human pets," Ismene said, shooting down Jarrett's suggestion.

"I thought Elson was the top dog…you know, the leader of all the vampires."

"He is. He's the constable, but he and Chaos have been friends for decades; they share a mutual respect."

"Are you saying that Sophia can do pretty much what she wants and doesn't have to worry about consequences?"

"It depends."

"On what?"

"Depends on which law she breaches. Look, it's complicated. Chaos told her to help us out with the blood drive campaign and she put in a lot of work."

"But she was supposed to help with the move this morning, yet she didn't even bother to show up. As important as this move was to Elson, I don't think he'd approve of Sophia's lack of commitment."

"Like I said, Chaos was doing us a favor by loaning out Sophia. She may have been busy this morning…you know, handling something for Chaos."

Jarrett sighed, realizing that the discussion wasn't going anywhere. "I'm starting to get the impression that I'm nothing more than your personal blood slave in the evening and during the day, I'm like, the hired help…only I don't get paid."

Ismene rolled her eyes toward the ceiling. "Here we go again! I thought you helped out because you love me and that you believe that vampires are superior to humans." Ismene sighed. "But, if you'd like to be put on the payroll, I can arrange that with Elson." She turned to leave, but Jarrett grabbed her wrist.

"Hey, I've been waiting all day to spend some time with you, so don't walk away just because you don't like something I've said."

Ismene glared at the hand that grasped her wrist. "Unhand me."

Jarrett released his grip. "I didn't mean to—"

"Excuse me, I need a drink," Ismene said, her eyes glancing around the parlor.

Jarrett tapped the left side of his neck. "I got what you need, baby." He hoped his offer, along with a smile, would be accepted as an apology for his childish outburst.

"Maybe later," Ismene said, and wove through the guests.

Sophia sidled up next to Jarrett, wearing a catty grin. "Hey, Sloan, you'll never guess where I've been sleeping?"

"Don't know and don't care."

"With Chaos," she blurted.

"That's old news." He turned his mouth down, clearly annoyed with Sophia.

"I've been sleeping with him during the day…inside his coffin."

"Huh?"

"We're getting like…super close, and he wants me near him at all times."

"Sounds real uncomfortable."

"No, I lie on top of Chaos, and with his arms wrapped around me, it's warm and intimate. I wouldn't be surprised if Chaos pops the question."

"That dude is wild and doesn't seem like he's ready to settle down. You're gonna get your feelings hurt if you think he's gonna ask you to marry him."

Sophia burst out laughing. "I'm not talking about marriage. I'm referring to a more permanent relationship—the kind that lasts forever."

Jarrett lifted a brow.

"I think he's gonna ask if I want to be a part of his family."

"Chaos doesn't have a family."

"I know, so if he turns me, I'll be his first—and I'll always have a special place in his heart. We'll be like Ismene and Elson."

"You're such a moron. Ismene and Elson don't sleep together—they're family." Jarrett's pitch rose and he felt himself burning with envy.

"Hey, get a grip, Sloan. It's not my fault that Ismene treats you like an indentured slave." She erupted in a cruel burst of laughter, and then strutted away.

Jarrett scanned the crowd and noticed Ismene sipping blood from a crystal chalice as she chatted with Mayor Ringwood. A fresh wave of jealousy rushed through him. The evening passed so quickly, it was annoying that Ismene would waste the few precious hours they could spend together, making small talk with the boring mayor.

Sophia was right; Ismene didn't care about him. She had never invited him to share her flower and sunshine-painted coffin, and he doubted if she was interested in getting that intimate with him. And since she'd made it clear that she didn't have the authority to turn him into a vampire, what was the point in continuing with their relationship? It was ironic that Sophia, the blood slut, was being treated with more dignity than Jarrett. Ismene took his devotion for granted, and he was getting sick and tired of continually moping around like a lovesick puppy.

Without bothering to say good night to anyone, Jarrett slipped out of the parlor and walked down the long corridor that led to the main entrance. As he exited the mansion, he noticed two police squad cars pulling up. The city jail was pretty much empty now that lawbreakers were immediately handed over to Elson.

CHAPTER 23

In no rush to get home to listen to his parents' innumerable complaints about him, Jarrett drove slowly, following the speed limit. A part of him wanted to turn his SUV around and go back to the party, but he realized that returning would reveal him to be as big of a chump as Ismene apparently thought he was. Women! Even dead ones were nothing but trouble.

Times like now, Jarrett could really use a friend. He'd heard that Holland Manning was back in town, but unfortunately, he'd deleted her number. He wondered if he'd be welcome if he showed up at her door, uninvited. The last time they'd spoken, she made it clear that she didn't hold a grudge against him. He toyed with the idea of popping up on Holland, and asking if she'd like to go for a ride. He finally decided that the only way to find out if they were still on speaking terms was to man-up and ring her doorbell.

His ex-girlfriend, Chaela Vasquez, had been high-maintenance and fiery. Ismene was moody and often sullen, and it would be a pleasant change to spend some time with an easy-going girl who would lend a sympathetic ear. Feeling extremely lonely, Jarrett found himself wondering if there was a chance that he and Holland could be more than friends. After Ismene's dizzying kisses, it would be weird making out with a regular girl—but it was something he'd have to get used to.

Excited by the prospect of getting together with Holland, Jarrett picked up speed. In the distance, he saw something stumbling around in the dark. It was odd to see anyone out after dark in Frombleton. Only a staggering drunk would be foolish enough to brave the night now that the vampires had made their presence known. Jarrett turned on his high beams to get a better look, and he let out a sound of surprise when he realized that the man was badly injured. *A bar fight?* Jarrett wondered as he noticed that blood was smeared over the man's clothing. There was a gaping wound on the back of his head, and rivulets of blood ran down his neck.

Had the vampires done that to the dude? Jarrett shook his head. That hole in dude's head didn't look like vampire work. Their bites were small punctures, not huge craters. It looked as if the poor fool had been attacked by a wild animal or maybe someone in the bar had wacked him in the back of the head with a golf club…or an ax. Curious to know what had happened, Jarrett honked his horn.

The bloody drunk swung around. Frothing at the mouth, he growled and hissed as he lumbered toward the SUV. The man seemed beyond drunk; there was something not quite human about him. The maniac flung himself on the hood of the Durango. He began pounding and scratching at the windshield, snapping his teeth as if trying to bite through the glass.

"What the—" Jarrett froze mid-sentence when the man began to grunt louder, his face contorted viciously. As he smashed through his windshield with his balled fists, there was a look of all-consuming hunger in his eyes.

"What's your problem? Get off my truck!" he shouted, honking his horn frantically. Trying to throw the drunken madman off the Durango, Jarrett shifted into reverse, pressed hard on the gas pedal, and then slammed on the brakes. Gripping the windshield wipers, the crazed man hung on.

Desperate to lose his unwanted passenger, Jarrett accelerated. When the odometer shot to one-twenty, he made a sharp, right turn. And then something happened. For a moment, it seemed as if he were suspended in time. The SUV was briefly airborne and then landed with a boom on its side. Somehow Jarrett found himself in the back seat, his breath coming in heaving gasps. It took a moment to become oriented enough to realize that the drunk was gone. Probably smashed beneath the wreckage or hurled headfirst into a telephone pole. Giddy with relief, he began to check himself for injuries. Amazingly, he didn't seem to have sustained even a tiny scratch.

But his sense of well-being was short-lived. The sound of shattering glass and determined grunting announced that the intruder had gained entry into the wrecked vehicle. Jarrett was stunned by that kind of endurance, especially from someone suffering from a serious head wound. What did the maniac want? Money? Jewelry? He wondered what kind of sicko would rob a victim of a car accident.

Maybe the drunk was one of the people he'd signed up for the blood drive, and maybe he was out for revenge. Serious revenge—like murder. Choked by terror, Jarrett coughed and cleared his throat. "What do you want, man? What do you want?" he repeated with tension crackling in his voice.

There was no intelligible response, only incomprehensible utterances and low, threatening growls. Sensing that the psycho wanted something other than money, Jarrett lunged for the door handle. With the car upside down, the handle was above his head. He stretched his arm, but he was too late.

There was an explosion of pain in his side—blinding agony

that dazed him. He initially thought he'd been stabbed deeply—like with a sword. But how would the crazy drunk suddenly get hold of a sword? Then a warm splash of blood hit Jarrett's face and a sloshing sound began to fill his ears. Filled with dread, he gazed downward and recoiled. "No!" he bellowed when he realized that the drunk was clinging to him, his jaws moving up and down as he chewed deeper into the open wound on Jarrett's side.

With horrifying clarity, Jarrett realized he hadn't been stabbed at all. The crazy drunk was actually eating him alive!

⊕ ⊕ ⊕

"Holland!" There was urgency in Phoebe's tone and Holland sat bolt upright.

"What's wrong—did I oversleep? I didn't hear the alarm go off."

"You didn't oversleep. Schools are closed until further notice. No one's allowed out except medical personnel and law enforcement."

"Whaaat?" Holland sat up and gawked at her mother. "What's going on?"

"There were several attacks last night…horrible murders."

"Vamps?"

Phoebe shook her head. "No, something else. The news reports are stating that they think the people were attacked by animals." Her mother paused, her eyes darting away.

"What is it, Mom?"

"One of the victims was a classmate of yours…that boy you were so crazy about."

"Jarrett Sloan?" Holland asked. Phoebe nodded and Holland buried her face in her hands. Phoebe sat on the bed and rubbed a circle in the middle of Holland's back.

Teary-eyed, Holland looked up. "Jarrett was so confused. So misguided. I've heard rumors that he's been hanging out and partying with the bloodsuckers, and he's been actually working for them."

"If he was working for vampires, wouldn't it be counter-productive for them to harm him?"

Holland shrugged. "Perhaps he no longer served a purpose. I don't know. I feel so bad for Jarrett. He was never the same after Zac continually blood-sucked him last summer. I hate vampires; they're all so evil and devious."

Phoebe's fingers absently grazed her neck, as if checking to see if her old puncture wounds were still there. Holland noticed the gesture. "I'm sorry, Mom. I didn't mean to remind you of... you know...what Zac did to you."

"I have no memory of Zac biting me, but I still feel guilty for trying to set you up with him."

"You didn't know he was a vampire; your heart was in the right place."

"The thought of what could have happened to you makes me shudder."

"Nothing would have happened to me—but Zac would have suffered a horrible death. Well...thanks to Jonas, he got what he deserved. Look, we survived Zac and that creepy vampire family, the Sullivans," Holland reminded.

"Yes, we did," Phoebe murmured. She narrowed her eyes in thought. "It doesn't make sense for Jarrett to embrace vampires after all that Zac put him through."

"I heard that Jarrett became sort of an outcast at school—kicked off the football team, scorned by his teammates and his peers. I know all too well how it feels to be an outsider. Maybe he was desperate to have friends and the vamps deceived him into believing that he belonged. God knows they're masters of deception."

Holland clicked on the TV in her room, but there was no picture or sound. She gave her mother a perplexed look. "Did you pay the cable bill?"

"Yeah, I saw the news report a few minutes ago, and my TV was just fine. I'll check and see if it's on the blink, too," she said, rising from Holland's bed. Holland slipped her feet into her slippers and trailed behind her mother. The TV in Phoebe's room was as dark and silent as Holland's.

"I don't know what's going on; I definitely paid the bill," Phoebe said, aiming the remote and surfing through the channels. "I'll call the cable company," she said, tossing the remote in disgust.

While her mother was on a lengthy hold with the cable provider, Holland pulled the curtain aside and gazed out the front window, wondering if the neighbors' cable was working okay. The sun was shining brightly. The streets were empty with no sounds of life. It looked like a peaceful day...too peaceful.

Craning her neck, she could see the mail carrier near the end of the block, going from house to house. She was relieved to see that Frombleton hadn't been shut down completely. School would probably be back in session tomorrow, and intending to make good use of this unexpected downtime, Holland decided to work on another spell. Something powerful enough to completely change Jonas back to his former self.

She stepped away from the window, but something caught her eye. Peering through the window with squinted eyes, she was stunned at what she saw. "Mom!" she yelled. "Mom, come quick."

Holding the phone, Phoebe hurried to the living room, and joined Holland at the window. "The mailman's acting weird," Holland said, pointing across the street. There was a trail of letters and small packages on the pavement and scattered on lawns. The mail carrier had made his way to the middle of the block, and was going door to door, lifting the lid of mailboxes, but instead of inserting mail, he tossed envelopes over his shoulder, and then angrily slammed the lid back down.

"Why's he doing that?" Holland inquired in a whispered voice. Phoebe scowled. "I have no idea."

"It's like he can't remember the procedure for delivering mail and his forgetfulness is infuriating him."

Moving on to the next few houses, the mail carrier was now directly across the street. His gait had become clumsy and unstable, and Holland gazed at her mother with furrowed brows. "Something's really wrong with him, Mom; look at the way he's walking."

Mr. Marricone from across the street swung his door open and stood in the doorframe wearing a bathrobe and yelling at the mail carrier. The mail carrier turned around and trudged back to Mr. Marricone's house, his slow movements and the way his head was hung low, suggested remorse.

Continuing ranting, it was apparent that Mr. Marricone didn't want an apology. "What's your problem, throwing mail all over the street? If you don't like your job, then get another one! With everything that's going on in this town, the last thing we need is a disgruntled postal worker," Mr. Marricone bellowed in a voice that was loud enough for Holland and her mother to hear. He mouthed off some more in a lower register, and they couldn't make out what he was saying.

With his mail sack slung haphazardly, the mail carrier suddenly lunged for Mr. Marricone, and grabbed his head with both hands.

Phoebe yelped in surprise. "My goodness; the postman's head butting Mr. Marricone; I have to call the police!"

Holding Mr. Marricone's face pressed against his, it appeared as if they were kissing really passionately. Mr. Marricone let out a loud, pained yowl, and Holland backed away from the window. "Hurry! Call the police! The mailman's going nuts, and it looks like he's biting Mr. Marricone's face."

CHAPTER 24

Phoebe looked at the phone in astonishment. "I'm getting a recorded message; it's saying that my call will be picked up in five minutes. Can you believe that?"

"Maybe there's a spike in calls…you know, like, maybe a lot of people are reporting the mailman's behavior."

There was another high-pitched yell—a female scream—that sent a chill up Holland's spine. Phoebe was rattled so badly, she dropped the phone. Phoebe and Holland ran to the window and were horrified to see Mr. Marricone sprawled out on his porch, his robe splayed open, and there was a dark substance that looked suspiciously like blood pooling around his head.

The mail carrier had gotten inside the Marricone house, arguing with Ms. Marricone. If one didn't know better, it would appear that their two silhouettes were engaged in a stirring ballroom dance. But, of course, they weren't dancing. They were struggling. And Ms. Marricone was yelling for help.

"We have to do something," Phoebe said, stooping down and picking up the phone. She jabbed the buttons again, and then scoffed in disbelief. "The line's still busy! This is ridiculous."

"Mr. Marricone's bleeding badly. What should we do, Mom?"

"I don't know," Phoebe confessed, brushing her hair out of her face and with a quavering hand she tried the call again, but getting the same recorded message, she hit the END CALL button and shook her head.

The screams inside the Marricone residence died down, and the mail carrier stumbled out of the house, looking around as if wondering what to do next. Suddenly, old Ms. Jaworski, the nosiest neighbor on the block, came running out of her house, wielding a broom.

"What's the matter with you, Patrick?" Ms. Jaworski demanded, calling the mail carrier by his first name. "What have you done to the Marricones? Have you lost your mind?" she shouted angrily.

"What did you do to Mr. Marricone?" she asked, pointing to Mr. Marricone's collapsed, bleeding body.

Holland and Phoebe stood at the window, their eyes wide with astonishment as they watched the mail carrier bare his teeth and respond with guttural sounds and animal-like growls. Ms. Jaworski swung the handle of the broom. Packages spilled from the mail sack, and envelopes swirled and floated in the air as the enraged mail carrier snatched Ms. Jaworski by her graying hair. He pulled her face close to his open mouth, and Ms. Jaworski began to squawk—ungodly sounds that ran the range of surprise, fury, and pain.

"I think he's biting her, Mom!" By now, Holland was standing on her tiptoes, trying to get a better look. Ms. Jaworski's screams were torturous sounds, and Phoebe desperately began pressing 9-1-1, trying to get help.

"I'm still getting that damned recorded message," she said bitterly.

From the houses across the street, Holland could see curtains fluttering open and shadowy images peeking through blinds. "Maybe there's a way to contact the police department online," Holland suggested in a fearful voice.

"Good idea. I'll check." Phoebe picked up her laptop from the coffee table.

An explosion of shattering glass caused Holland to jump.

"What was that?" Phoebe said in a strained voice.

"He smashed the Woodward family's window, and I can't believe it, but he's climbing through the broken window, forcing his way into their house."

"What's the matter with you; get out of here!" someone in the Woodward household shrieked.

"Are you serious?" Phoebe rushed to the window and yanked the curtain closed. "Get away from the window; we don't want him to know we're in here." She grabbed Holland's hand. "Come on, hon; we're staying in the basement until the police get here."

Heading for the basement, Phoebe and Holland froze momentarily when they heard a fresh chorus of screams and roars. Phoebe pulled Holland along, and then opened the basement door. "Downstairs, Holland. Hurry!"

⊕ ⊕ ⊕

The basement was unfinished with exposed pipes, a cement floor, and concrete walls. Besides being the place where the washer and dryer were stored, the basement was also the stockpile area for everything from old furniture to dusty boxes filled with family pictures.

Holland and Phoebe sat huddled together on a three-legged sofa, both too shocked to speak. Holland's mind was reeling with the unbelievably grotesque images she'd seen. "He bit them," she murmured incredulously. "I saw the mailman bite Ms. Jaworski and Mr. Marricone, and they're dead."

"You don't know that, Holland. They could both be unconscious...or dazed."

He killed them! I couldn't see what he was doing to Mrs.

Marricone, but I think she's dead, too. What would make a person go crazy like that?" Holland asked as she anxiously twisted her pajama top sleeve.

Phoebe had no response; all she could do was shake her head.

"Do you think it's possible that it was the mailman and not wild animals that attacked those people last night?"

"Jesus, I hope not."

Holland and Phoebe sat quietly for a few moments until they were jolted by the sudden and persistent sound of a car alarm. Holland stared at her mother with a gaping mouth. "What's he doing now—deliberately knocking into someone's car?"

The honking car horn created a domino effect, and a series of car alarms began to go off. Phoebe tightened her hand around Holland's. "Where are the police—don't they hear this commotion?"

There was the unmistakable siren wail of a burglar alarm, and Holland cringed. "He's breaking into one house after another; we can't sit on our hands down here in the basement," Holland said, staring with frightened eyes at the small basement window on the other side of the room.

Phoebe wrapped an arm around Holland. "There're bars on that window. We're safe down here, hon."

"But…but, suppose he gets in through the living room window, and you know…and comes down here looking for us?"

"I don't think he's gonna make it to our house. It seems like he's following his mail route and I'm sure the police will be here before he works his way to our side of the street."

"But suppose they don't come."

"They will!"

Holland shot her mother a look of terror as frightened shrieks and inarticulate shouting grew nearer; it sounded as if a number of people had poured out into the street.

"I need to know what's going on." Holland jumped up and dragged a stepladder over to the basement window that was rather high-up. Holland motioned for her mother to come take a look.

Stunned by what she'd seen, Holland took shaky steps down the ladder. Phoebe climbed up. She peeped out the miniscule window and cringed. "Oh, no!" she gasped.

Many of their neighbors from the opposite side of the street had run out of their homes in an attempt to get away from the raging mail carrier. Their neighborhood looked like Armageddon, with numerous injured people, many in their pajamas and bath-robes, holding up bloodied arms or cupping their bleeding faces and necks as they sought shelter inside cars and behind bushes and trees. Some were walking in dazed circles while others lay bloodied and crumpled out on their lawns and on the pavement.

The mail carrier was no longer in view, but judging from the sounds of breaking glass, alarms wailing, and people screaming, he was still on a biting rampage. Holland wondered if Jonas could possibly have anything to do with what was happening. *No!* There were others like Jonas, but they weren't in Frombleton, and they certainly weren't government workers, delivering mail. Jonas had described them as barely human creatures, not responsible citizens holding down jobs.

Furthermore, as recent as yesterday, the mailman had been perfectly okay. Holland remembered seeing him on her way to school—they'd exchanged hellos. Whatever had caused him to go berserk had nothing to do with Jonas. Yet, it seemed like such an odd coincidence—strange animal attacks last night and now this. She couldn't shake the nagging doubt in her mind.

She hated to admit it, but the savage way the mailman grabbed Mr. Marricone and Ms. Jaworski reminded her of how Jonas had attacked Headmistress Livingston when he rescued her from

Stoneham. What would Jonas say when she told him that the mailman had stormed her street and had viciously bitten and possibly killed several neighbors? She needed to find out if he would be as shocked as her, or would there be a guilty silence between them.

Phoebe came down from the ladder, her face a grim mask. "It's bedlam out there."

"Do you have the house phone?" Holland asked her mother.

"No, it's upstairs," Phoebe said, shaking her head.

"My cell phone's upstairs, too. I have to get it." Holland turned around and her mother grabbed her by the arm.

"I'm not letting you risk your life to make a phone call. You are going to sit tight until the police have carted that maniac off to jail."

"But…but, I really need to call Jonas," she said in a pleading tone.

"No! You're not thinking straight. You're gonna sit tight and wait until the police arrive," Phoebe said adamantly, her voice escalating. Holland was usually the voice of reason; she was usually the one nudging her mother in the right direction…but not today.

Their disagreement was interrupted by the welcomed sounds of sirens. "Thank God!" Phoebe said. "We can go upstairs now."

Holland let out a breath of relief and raced up the stairs. Keeping pace, Phoebe was right behind her. At the top of the stairs, Holland sped to her bedroom and Phoebe hurried to the living room window.

Holland tried Jonas's cell twice without success, and then called the main number of The Atwell. To her surprise, her call to the hotel went to voicemail. Did the hotel shut down, too? Wearing a confused expression, she wandered into the living room.

"What's going on?" she said as she joined her mother at the window.

"It's the strangest thing. The EMT guys were loading the injured people into the ambulance, and from what I could tell, the police seemed to be getting statements from the crowd. All of a sudden, two people broke out into a fight, and then someone else dove into the fray. All three ended up in handcuffs and thrown in a cruiser."

Holland gazed out and noticed that a few people were outside milling about. No doubt, they were discussing the terrible events. "What about the mailman—did they get him?"

"I would imagine. Three ambulances went one way and the police cars sped in the opposite direction with their lights flashing. It's quiet now, so they must have apprehended him." Phoebe walked toward the door. "I'm going outside to find out what everyone knows."

Holland nodded, but her thoughts were focused on Jonas.

CHAPTER 25

Holland changed from her PJs into jeans and a pullover sweater. While her mother was outside gossiping with the neighbors, Holland retrieved the ancient spell book from beneath folded sweaters on a shelf in her bedroom closet. Today's awful events gave her a sense of urgency, and she desperately needed to work on a new spell for Jonas, and something to free the town from the curse. She had bookmarked the Hex-Removal spell, but she needed to find something more powerful to completely free Jonas from the curse. Sitting on her bed, Holland turned the pages, but the book was so thick, and contained so many different spells, she didn't know where to begin.

Suddenly her phone jingled next to her. Practically hyperventilating from excitement, she picked up the phone and checked out the screen. Seeing Rebecca's name, Holland groaned in disappointment. "Hello," she said with less than enthusiasm.

"Are you okay, Holland?" Rebecca asked anxiously.

"I guess."

"What do you mean, you guess? I heard about what happened on your street; have you or your mom been bitten?"

"No! We're fine. What's going on, Rebecca?"

After a deep intake of breath, Rebecca said, "You're not going to like this, Holland."

"What?" Holland said in shaky voice.

"I believe that Jonas is responsible for this biting epidemic. Last night, authorities were placing the blame on wild animals, but now there's been a series of biting incidents all over the city—people from all walks of life are suddenly attacking and biting each other. No one knows what to make of it, but this has something to do with Jonas and that curse."

"It can't be; Jonas has never bitten anyone in Frombleton. He had a few mishaps in other towns, but he's controlling the situation…you know, as best he can."

"Obviously, he's not controlling anything, with all the bloodshed and mayhem that's occurring in Frombleton."

"There're maybe a dozen or so, uh, creatures that he may have accidently…um…sired, but he's been containing them at a location where they can't hurt anyone."

"Whatever he created has spread to Frombleton and it couldn't be happening at a more inopportune time. The vampires are taking over this city, and I don't know how my coven is going to manage this new, unimaginable outbreak at the same time that we're dealing with them. Look, your house is protected from the vampires at night, but you're free game for the police and those flesh-eaters during the day."

"What do you mean, we're free game for the police? The police are helping to keep things under control."

"No, they're not. They're working for the vampires, taking humans to the vampire nest."

But…but I saw them across the street from my house…helping."

"They're pretending to help. Listen, I want you and your mom to drive to the old armory across town. My coven and I are staying there and we're putting a force field around the building in exactly one hour. Of course, you can walk through the force field at any time…but your mother can't. She has to get here ASAP!"

"But what about Jonas? He needs me, and I can't abandon him now."

"One hour, Holland," Rebecca said firmly. "Don't put your mother's life at risk."

She had to save her mother from whatever was going on in Frombleton. Heartbroken that she had to leave without seeing or talking to Jonas, Holland plodded from her bedroom to the living room. She opened the front door just in time to see a fight breaking out between—of all people—her shy, gangly neighbor, thirteen-year-old Roger Hales, and nice Mr. Davidson, who enjoyed bird-watching. It was surreal to see sweet Roger with his face contorted in rage as he yelled and threw blows. And plump Mr. Davidson's lips were curled viciously as he pounded scrawny Roger with his beefy fists.

Mr. Davidson had Roger by at least a hundred pounds, and what would have ordinarily been an unfair fight had strangely become an even match, with the teen and the older man equally outraged and each holding his own.

"Get away from them, Mom," Holland yelled, running toward her mother, who, along with Ms. Furman from around the corner, was trying to separate Roger and Mr. Davidson, and pleading with them to get a grip and to calm down.

As Holland got closer, she could hear that Roger and Mr. Davidson weren't making much sense; they were both yelling angrily, but weren't speaking actual words. The sounds they produced were nothing more than rage-filled gibberish.

Holland pulled her mother forcibly, and in the nick of time. The next howl of pain came from Ms. Furman, as Roger and Mr. Davidson inexplicably turned on her. Like two beasts from the wild, they attacked Ms. Furman. Roger's teeth were locked on her shoulder, and Mr. Davidson was ripping into her back, pulling her down to the ground.

Holland and Phoebe ran screaming into their house, and the onlookers scattered in all directions, yelling for help.

From the safety of their home, Holland and her mother hugged each other. "My God, what's happening to everyone?" Phoebe asked.

"Rebecca called. She said people are going nuts all over town. She wants us to drive to the old armory. Her coven is staying there until this is over."

"Okay, grab some snacks from the kitchen while I pack an overnight bag for us."

"We don't have time. Just pack something to sleep in, in case we have to stay overnight. They're putting up a force field in less than hour. The drive is gonna take about forty minutes, so we have to leave now."

Phoebe nodded. My keys are in the bedroom," she said, and trotted down the hall. Holland trekked to her own room, threw on a jacket and crammed pajamas and her laptop into the backpack she used for school. She placed the ancient spell book into a separate compartment.

Back in the living room, she saw her mother standing at the window, a hand covering her mouth. "Ms. Furman," she uttered, recoiling at the sight and shaking her head.

"Are Roger and Mr. Davidson still out there?" Holland asked.

"No, they've moved on. Come on, let's go."

Racing to the Saab, Phoebe warned, "Keep moving, Holland; don't look at Ms. Furman."

Holland tried her best to keep her eyes straight ahead, but she couldn't help from stealing a glance. And what she saw took her breath away. All that was left of Ms. Furman was the shredded remains of her clothes, a blood-stained necklace, bones, hair, and gore.

Phoebe backed the Saab out of the driveway and collided with a plastic trash can that had rolled from someone's yard. Looking through the back window, Holland saw Roger violently kicking his own front door, and she assumed his family wouldn't let him in. She couldn't blame them. Mr. Davidson was not in her line of vision, but she could hear his distinct, anger-driven, deep-toned gibberish.

Phoebe picked up speed, and out of nowhere a pink blur appeared. "Jesus Christ!" Phoebe shouted and slammed on the brakes. Four-year-old Kylie Rutherford, whom Holland had babysat occasionally, was wandering in the street. Wearing pink pajamas with the word PRINCESS imprinted on the front in sparkly, swirled letters, the little girl was holding the side of her head, and murmuring unhappily.

"Is she okay? Did I hit her?" Phoebe said in a voice rising with hysteria. She quickly shifted into park and opened her door.

"You didn't hit her! She's okay. Don't get out, Mom. I...I'm not sure if we should uh, trust her," Holland stammered.

"She's a helpless little kid, for goodness sake. We can't leave her alone in the street."

"Mom, please. Don't get out of the car. Let me handle this." Holland slid down her window. "Hey, Kylie," she said in a gentle tone. "What are you doing out here by yourself—where are your mom and dad?"

Kylie's hand fell away from her head, revealing fingers sticky with blood and a ragged hole on the side of her head. Holland screamed, and Phoebe gaped in disbelief. Kylie's upper lip curled into a snarl as she advanced toward the car. "She's bitten! Pull off, Mom; let's go!"

Phoebe took off with a lurch and a skid, broadsiding several parked cars in her haste to get away. "Someone bit out a chunk of that child's head. My God, they're even biting little kids!"

Holland recalled what Rebecca had said about people from all walks of life attacking each other. Could Jonas actually be responsible for such widespread devastation?

They got out of Holland's neighborhood without any other altercations, but when they reached downtown Frombleton, they discovered that Edgemont Avenue was clogged with traffic, and many people were running and screaming in terror.

"What's happening now?" Phoebe said, gawking in astonishment at the people that were stampeding in the street and on the sidewalk.

"Everyone's running that way," Holland said pointing behind her. "Maybe we should turn around and go back home."

"Make up your mind," Phoebe snapped. "You rushed me out of the house to get to Rebecca's safe place, and now you want me to turn around?"

"Yeah, I think we should." Holland surveyed the traffic jam; all the cars on both sides of the street had stopped moving.

Phoebe backed up a little, and Holland turned around, motioning for the car behind them to back up and give them a little room. Instead of backing up, the driver inched closer.

Phoebe sighed in exasperation. "I can't turn around; they've got me boxed in."

"Drive on the pavement; do whatever you have to do to. We shouldn't sit in traffic while people are running in the opposite direction," Holland said, her head poked out the window, trying to see what was causing the traffic jam.

Split seconds later, a swarm of people with repulsive, dead eyes, and rotting flesh stormed down Edgemont Avenue. The gruesome crowd swiftly descended on a white Chevy Malibu. Trying to get to the unfortunate family that was trapped inside the vehicle, the monstrous horde grunted and drooled as they pounded against metal and glass with tremendous force. A cacophony of shattering glass and chilling screams filled the air as they broke through the car windows and began clawing at the people inside.

While the unbelievable horror unfolded, more and more people scrambled out of their cars, leaving keys in the ignitions and engines running as they fled in different directions.

"We have to run, Mom," Holland shouted. Frozen with fear, Phoebe sat with her hands wrapped around the steering wheel.

"Mom, let's go!" She clenched her mother's shoulder, and shook her as hard as she could. Jolted into attentiveness, Phoebe scooted over and followed Holland out of the passenger's side. No sooner had their feet hit the asphalt when approximately half of the drooling monsters abandoned the Chevy and came after them.

CHAPTER 26

Holland and Phoebe ran as fast as they could. Looking wildly to the left and right, Holland shouted, "This way, Mom!" and veered to the right, turning onto a small, deserted street.

Holland and Phoebe ran aimlessly for at least ten minutes before they stopped to catch their breath. "Ohmigod, ohmigod, ohmigod," Phoebe said over and over, holding her chest and panting. "What are those *things?* The mailman, Roger, and Mr. Davidson...even little Kylie—they were all acting violent and crazy, but they looked very much alive. But those *things* on Edgemont Avenue...their bodies were decaying, and the sounds they were making didn't seem human at all. What could have caused them to change into living corpses?"

Holland shrugged, but she knew the answer. That rabid mob of corpses were the creatures that Jonas was trying to protect and shelter. *How can he possibly believe they have any redeeming qualities?* Holland wondered, horrified. They were obviously dead, responding only to the movement and the scent of blood. Holland was certain that the corpses and not wild animals had killed Jarrett Sloan and the others last night, and there was no telling how many others they'd eaten alive.

A nearby explosion of gunshots created a calamitous roar. More screaming, more pounding footfalls as people ran for cover. Holding their heads, Holland and Phoebe dropped to the ground. "Are they shooting at us now?" Phoebe asked in a trembling voice.

"I don't think those creatures are capable of firing a weapon."

Two more shots were fired and these sounded extremely close. Phoebe covered her face with her hands, and a strangled sob tore from her throat. "This is insane. We'd be better off if we'd stayed in the basement."

Holland couldn't disagree, and she felt responsible for taking them out of the safety of their home. "We can make it back home, Mom. We're only a few miles away."

Phoebe looked around, taking in her surroundings. "No, we're at least ten miles from home, and that's pretty far when you're on foot, ducking gunshots and killer corpses."

A car roared behind them, and tires squealed as the car came to a stop. Holland and Phoebe whirled around and both blinked in surprise at the sight of a police squad car. Phoebe let out a long sigh of relief, while Holland stared at the vehicle suspiciously. There were two people in the back and someone else sat up front, next to the police officer, but Holland couldn't make out their faces.

"You ladies okay? Have you been bitten?" the officer asked, brown eyes narrowed as he scrutinized them. He was a handsome guy with a quick smile, but his good looks and easy smile didn't fool Holland.

"We're okay; we haven't been bitten," Holland said warily.

"Get in; I'll take you to a safe place," the cop said, offering a wider smile that was meant to put them at ease. He got out of the car and slowly approached them. Holland noticed he was all brawn and muscle; the kind of guy that seemed perfectly capable of rescuing her and Phoebe.

"Thank God you're here," Phoebe exclaimed. "Those walking

corpses are terrorizing people on Edgemont Avenue—where did they come from?"

"We don't know, ma'am, but we're handling the situation as best we can."

Phoebe nodded eagerly. "Good, good. We were trying to get to the old armory—"

Remembering Rebecca's comment that the police were helping the vampires, Holland grasped her mother's hand. "Shh, don't give out information," she scolded in a whisper, and then began backing away. "Thanks, officer; we're okay. We're close to home; we can walk," Holland said, her eyes darting back and forth.

Phoebe shot Holland a look of bewilderment. "Are you nuts? Of course, we need a ride; all hell is breaking loose around us!"

"Which is it—home or the armory?" the cop asked, his eyes darkening with suspicion.

"The armory," Phoebe blurted. She glanced at Holland. "Sorry, hon, but the only way we're going to get there is under police protection."

Holland groaned. Her mom could be such a ditz sometimes, and whenever she slipped into kook mode, Holland had to assume the role of parent. Phoebe couldn't have chosen a more inappropriate time to place blind faith into a man merely because he was wearing a badge and a uniform.

The cop eyed Phoebe. "Why're you headed for the old armory? It's shut down, and I don't have any information about the place being used as an emergency shelter."

"We've been through a lot and she's confused; like I said, we're going home." Holland squeezed her mother's hand, silently pleading for her to please stop talking.

The cop looked at Phoebe. "What's your address, ma'am? I have orders to assist all citizens. Now, I need you ladies to get in the car and come with me," he said gruffly. His patient smile had been replaced with something that resembled a sneer.

"We're not going with you!" Holland shouted and then squeezed her eyes closed and began softly chanting a short, Latin incantation that she'd memorized—just in case.

The cop gawked at Holland. "Is she okay…you know, up here?" he asked, tapping his temple with the pad of his finger.

Phoebe shrugged embarrassedly. "She has these spells sometimes."

His eyes shifted to Holland, whose lips were moving so fast, they seemed to be trembling, and the drone of her voice sounded similar to the soft buzz of bees inside a hive. "What kind of spell is she having?" the cop demanded.

Phoebe held out her hands in a gesture of helplessness. "You know, an ordinary spell."

"What's an ordinary spell? Is she going into a seizure—what's wrong with her?" He sounded irritated as if having to deal with an illness was a huge inconvenience. "Look, she's freaking me out…you two can get going," the cop said disgustedly, and turned around.

But instead of taking steps toward the squad car, he began teetering back and forth, arms stretched out at his sides and one leg lifting slightly as he struggled to keep his balance.

"Are you all right, officer?" Phoebe inquired.

"What's she doing to me?" he yelled. "Make her stop!" He took another unsteady step, and sweat poured down his face. "Let me off this thing!" he yelled.

"What thing?" Phoebe asked, while Holland continued chanting.

"She's got me up in the air; I'm on a tightrope. Let me off; I wanna get down!" he hollered.

Holland went quiet and opened her eyes. The cop's face had

gone pale, and he wore a look of utter terror as he propelled his arms, trying to stay atop the imaginary tight rope. Holland opened the front door of the squad car. "Listen carefully. I assume you all escaped the madness on Edgemont Avenue, and you believed that the cop was going to take you to a safe place—well, he wasn't. He works for the vampires, and he intended to deliver you to them."

The three people in the police car all gazed at Holland with looks of surprise on their faces. Holland smiled wryly. "The whispers and rumors you've been hearing about vampires are all true. Vampires are as real as those walking corpses on Edgemont Avenue."

A woman with a buzz haircut emerged from the front seat. She took a moment to glance at the cop who was struggling to stand upright before turning her attention to Holland. "Okay, I get that there are walking corpses in Frombleton. I barely escaped their attack on Edgemont Avenue. I've been hearing talk about vampires and I'm open-minded enough to accept that they exist." She pointed to the cop. "But this thing you're doing to him—is it mind control—hypnosis? I mean, wow! Look at him—he really believes he's teetering high above ground. What did you to him and *what* are you?" She stared at Holland, probing her with her piercing, brown eyes.

"I'm a witch. A good witch—most of the time."

Two young men in the back seat got out. They were college age, and one seemed like the studious type with glasses and inquisitive eyes, while the other was basketball-height tall, and gave off the air that most jocks emanated.

"So much has happened, and we don't know what to believe any longer," the guy with glasses said. "We don't know what to do or where to go. We woke up to dudes in the dorm going on biting rampages, and we were lucky to escape. We were trying to get out of Frombleton when we got caught up on Edgemont Avenue." He shook his head at the gruesome memory. "Those people…those monsters, or whatever they are, were ripping into motorists with their teeth. We had to ditch our car and run, and the police officer was our only hope of getting to a safe place.

"But now, he can't help us because you've got him out of his mind, believing he's doing some sort of high-wire act." All three squad car passengers cut an eye at the cop, who now was crouching with one foot kicked out in front of him, his arms unevenly outstretched as he fought to keep his balance.

"As if those zombie creatures weren't bad enough, we have to be worried about vampires harassing us at night—and witches flying on brooms." The buzz cut woman shook her head doubtfully. "It's too much to deal with. It's just so absurd; it's almost laughable."

"I know it sounds crazy. But I advise you all to find shelter. That cop was going to take you to the vampires and turn you into blood slaves."

"What's a blood slave?" the jock asked.

Holland sighed. "A blood slave is a person that's forced to provide the vamps with blood on a routine basis."

"Sounds painful," the jock said, scowling as his hand went up to his neck protectively.

"I hear it's very painful," Holland warned. "So stick together and hole up in one of these empty buildings until a rescue team gets here."

"When will that be?" Buzz cut wanted to know.

Holland shrugged. "I have no idea."

"We heard you tell the officer that you're headed for the armory; why can't we go with you?"

"You're welcome to come along," Phoebe piped in.

"Witches only," Holland said regretfully, wrapping an arm around her mother and guiding her away.

"Hey, you can't leave me up here like this," the cop yelled. "Let me off of this thing!"

"It's all in your head, man," the jock said. "You're not on anything; your feet are on the ground. The witch chick is using something like Jedi mind tricks to get you to do crazy stuff."

The cop's eyes briefly shot down to his feet. He gasped and squeezed his eyes shut. "I'm afraid of heights; I can't look down."

"You're bad off, dude," Buzz cut said. "Seeing as though you can't get off of whatever you think you're on, we're going to borrow your car…take some back roads to get ourselves to safety."

"You're stealing police property," the cop grumbled.

"Sorry, man. We're only borrowing it."

The trio of buzz cut, the jock, and the scholar piled back into the squad car, and pulled off with Buzz cut behind the wheel.

As Phoebe and Holland walked along the quiet street, Phoebe looked over her shoulder at the cop that thought he was walking a tightrope "What was that all about, Holland? Where'd you learn that spell you used on the policeman?"

"Something I picked up at Stoneham." Technically, she wasn't telling a lie. She'd obtained the ritual from The Book of Spells, and she would have never gotten access to so many ancient rituals had it not been for her experiences at Stoneham.

"Mom, we're closer to the armory than home. We should try to make it there. Being with Rebecca and her coven seems so much safer than being alone in our basement."

"You said we only had an hour to get there. We're too late."

"It doesn't matter. I can get through the force field, and I'll hold it open for you."

"Okay, but...what about those corpses? How are we going to get past them?"

"They seem to be congregated in the Edgemont Avenue vicinity. We can avoid them if we stay off the main streets."

"We should have accepted the ride in the police car," Phoebe griped.

"It seemed risky. They'll be in a world of trouble if they bump into that cop's brothers in blue. Besides, you're enough of a handful," Holland said with a sardonic smile. "I'm not capable of taking care of three additional people."

"How am I a handful?"

"Mom, you blabbed about the armory, giving the cop the exact location of a coven of witches that are secretly trying to take down the vampires. I don't know how I'm gonna break that news to Rebecca, but she needs to know. She may want to move the coven somewhere else, to be on the safe side."

"Sorry. I thought we could trust a police officer. I had no way of knowing he's working for vampires." Phoebe looked over her shoulder again, and in the far distance, she could see the blurry figure of the cop, inching along the imaginary tightrope. "How long is he going to be on that thing?" Phoebe asked.

"No idea. First time doing that spell."

CHAPTER 27

"What do you mean, no one showed up?" Elson raged at Ismene.

"The police brought in about twenty people while we slept during the day, but our regular donors didn't show up."

"Well, send someone to get them. And make sure they're punished appropriately."

"It's not that simple."

"Why isn't it?"

"We don't know where they are."

"Is this a joke?"

"No, Elson. Something's going on out there. The humans are being attacked by some sort of flesh-eaters."

Elson looked shocked. "Flesh-eaters?" he repeated in a tone of disbelief.

"I know it sounds crazy. I didn't believe it either. I sent Travis out with Walsh and Canelli. He'll be back soon with a report of his findings."

"Where's your pet? The boy, Jarrett?"

"I don't know. I've tried to penetrate his thoughts, but I'm hitting a blank wall."

"That's odd."

"I agree."

"Are you concerned?" Elson studied her face.

"No, not really. He can be replaced."

"Good to know. For a moment, I thought you were falling for the young jock." Elson laughed mockingly.

"He thought so, too," Ismene said with a devious smile.

"I've been thinking. We need to reach the people of Frombleton in a more efficient manner. Having our people go door to door is time-consuming."

"What do you propose?"

"Tell the mayor that I want names, addresses, and phone numbers of all the registered voters in the city."

"All right; I'll take care of that right away." Ismene turned to leave Elson's suite.

"Having the list of registered voters is going to keep us pretty busy. We're going to need help. I want that lawyer, Bradley, to run things here at the mansion during the day. I need someone with maturity, intelligence, and business savvy. Get him on the phone and tell him I want to see him ASAP. Oh, and send someone to pick up his daughter. We'll need to use her as leverage."

The ding of the elevator sounded, and Elson and Ismene moved through the suite and out into the wide corridor. The doors glided open and Travis stepped out. His face, hair, and his vest were speckled with blood.

"Did you stop for snacks on the way home?" Elson asked sarcastically.

"No. I have bad news." Travis dropped his head.

"What is it?" Elson's voice rose in agitation.

"It's Walsh and Canelli. They're both gone."

"Gone where?" Elson stepped forward, his eyes flamed.

"Those *things* got them."

"The flesh-eaters?" Ismene asked.

"Yeah, they pounced on the detectives, and left behind nothing but bones."

"Did they attack you?" Elson inquired.

"No, I'm swift. The minute I saw what happened to the two cops, I zipped myself right out of harm's way." A cocky grin flickered across Travis's face, and then his somber expression quickly returned.

Elson stroked his chin as he pondered Travis's report. "What are these flesh-eaters, and where'd they come from?"

"No idea, but there's a lot of 'em, and they seem to be hell-bent on eating up the whole town."

"What's your definition of a lot?"

Travis looked toward the ceiling and gave a whistle. "I'm guessing about a couple hundred."

"That's not so many. Forget about the humans tonight. We have enough stored blood to last us for months. Tonight, I'm officially waging war against these flesh eaters. I'll show them that they cannot storm into town and deplete our food supply. We're going to kill them all!"

"Uh, I don't know about killing them. I got the impression that they're already dead," Travis said. "They don't appear to possess any intelligence. They're motivated by hunger and respond to the scent of blood. The minute they smell the scent of warm, human blood, they start grunting and snapping their jaws."

"Hmm. We're dead also, but we can still be destroyed. Nothing is invincible. All we have to do is figure out what it takes to put them down for good."

"Well, it's not sunlight. Those snappers have been roaming the streets since last night without cease. Gunfire doesn't kill them either. I saw a man take a shot at several of them. They fall down but they get back up, hungrier than ever."

"You say that you zipped yourself out of their grasp, am I right?"

Travis nodded.

"Is it possible that they weren't trying to attack you?"

"Yeah, it's possible."

Elson grew quiet again. His head bowed as if in prayer, he telepathically summoned his family. Heeding his silent call, within minutes, Elson's children had come together and were congregated at the landing at the top of the grand staircase.

"As you are well aware, our human chattel didn't show up tonight. I initially thought they were being obstinate, but I've discovered that they're under attack by a strange and brutal force that devours human flesh and blood, leaving only bones." There were angry murmurings, and Elson paused, scanning the faces of the vampires that stood clustered together, hissing like snakes and muttering profanities at the news that their food source had been stolen from them.

"A lot of work went into organizing and training our humans to surrender their blood." Elson went silent. He tented his fingers and regarded his family. "Are we going to stand for this? Are we going to let a pack of brain-dead killers rob us of our only source of survival?" Elson cried in a voice that vibrated with rage.

"No!" the crowd of vampires roared in unison.

"You're right," Elson said, lowering his voice to a soft pitch. "We're going to rid this town of these fiends and then we'll celebrate." He turned toward Travis. "I want you to gather weapons, and take ten of your siblings out with you. I don't want you to take any humans with you; they'll attract the flesh eaters with their scent. Bring back the heads of no less than twenty of these flesh eaters."

Ismene stepped forward, ready to join Travis, but Elson seized her hand. "No! I need you here, by my side."

"But I'm a warrior; I should be leading the battle!"

"Do not disagree with me…ever," Elson said between clenched teeth.

"I apologize, Elson." Ismene stepped back. Disappointment creased the features of her face as she watched Travis and the other vampires storming toward the elevator.

Elson waved his arm. "The rest of you, head down to the artillery room and begin assembling the weapons." As the group of vampires hurried down the staircase, Elson looked upon Ismene. "Disagreeing with me in front of your siblings won't be tolerated. Such disrespect warrants a severe punishment."

"I know," she said, her head hung low.

"But…because I understand your passion for battle, I'm going to give you a pass—this once, but if you ever forget your place again, you'll find yourself outside, tethered to a tree when the sun rises." Elson stared at Ismene with burning eyes, and then the twin flames dimmed and his gaze softened. "Now, come, let's share a glass of chilled blood." He reached out and smiled when he felt her cool hand slip into his.

⊕ ⊕ ⊕

Travis and the other vampire warriors returned an hour later, covered in blood and gore and carrying sacks filled with severed heads. Elson enthusiastically rifled through the bags, retrieving one head after another, lining them in a row on a long wooden table. "How did you accomplish this?" he asked in an excited voice.

"It was easy. Chopping off their heads is a surefire way of exterminating those buggers. They don't get back up once their head has been severed. You were right, Elson. Taking humans along is a huge mistake. The second those snappers smell blood, they go into attack mode. But we vampires were able to walk right up on them without being detected. I have no doubt that we could end this plague tonight if we had a larger army."

Elson furrowed his brow. "Why do we need a larger army if slaughtering them is easy?"

"They're multiplying fast. Judging from what I saw, if they take a bite out of a human, within about fifteen minutes or so, the human becomes ravenous, and the next thing you know, he's snarling and snapping, too." Travis motioned to the row of severed heads. "Look at 'em. Some of them have rotted so bad, they look worse than death. Others look as alive as you or me."

"We're not alive, Travis," Ismene reminded.

"True, but we give the illusion of life. We can mingle among the living, and we don't have decaying skin, nor do we give off a telltale deathly stench."

Elson rubbed his hands together. "Good job, Travis, but there's still lots of work to be done. I've called on Chaos; he's on his way over to lend a hand, but as you know, his group is small. We have to figure out a way to cut down as many of those creatures as possible before the sun rises."

"May I make a suggestion?" Ismene asked.

Elson arched a brow and then nodded.

"Travis pointed out that the vampires were able to sneak up on the flesh eaters, undetected, so why not use human bait to attract them in larger numbers. While they're busy feasting on the human, we begin our attack, swiftly beheading an entire group instead of seeking them out, one at a time."

"Brilliant idea, Ismene," Elson said with a gleam in his eyes.

Travis grunted in displeasure. "Ismene's idea is not very original. I studied the behavior of those snappers when they attacked Walsh and Canelli."

"You were too busy zipping out of harm's way to study anything," Ismene shot back.

Travis raked his hair out his face and glowered at Ismene. "Hey, it's not my fault that you have to stay home and embroider, so don't take it out on me."

"You're too stupid to even keep up with the times. Women stopped embroidering as a pastime over a century ago."

Elson clenched his forehead wearily. "Ismene! Travis! This sibling rivalry between you two has grown tiresome; are you ever going to outgrow it?"

The doorbell rang, its haunting melody filling the historic mansion. "Ah, my comrade has arrived." Elson signaled for Lisette to go to the formal guest entry and greet Chaos.

"While I'm bringing Chaos up to speed, I'd like for Florencia to gather the human bait and oversee their transfer from the basement to the back of the vans," Elson told Ismene.

"I'll speak to Florencia right away."

"After you've given Florencia her instruction, I want you to join Chaos and me here, in the main room; I'd like to hear more of your ideas. I want the rest of you to fortify yourselves with blood before you go out to battle."

"Packaged blood or fresh?" Travis inquired.

"By all means, help yourselves to the fresh blood of the humans we have in bondage. We wouldn't want to let all that warm blood be guzzled up by those dreadful savages, would we?"

Unlike his usual exuberant self, Chaos entered the main room of the mansion wearing a troubled expression, and walking sluggishly with his shoulders slouched liked an old man. Elson gestured toward a chair, and Chaos let out a miserable groan, as if the act of sitting required great effort.

"You've heard about the trouble in Frombleton," Elson said.

"Yeah, I know about it, firsthand. Sophia went home last night to get a change of clothing. She was attacked and bitten, but she got away. When she came back, she had a big ol' chunk of meat bitten out of the back of her neck. She told me a crazy man had attacked her. I tried to clean the wound; I tried to seal it with my tongue, but nothing worked.

"She was in pain and I gave her a heavy dose of Oxy—knocked her out. When I woke up tonight, she was in my coffin with me, freaking out—yelling for me to let her out so she could go out and bite somebody."

Ismene joined them. "Good evening, Chaos. Would you care for a glass of blood?"

Chaos waved his hand, declining the offer.

"Please continue," Elson encouraged Chaos.

"I don't know what those things are that did that to Sophia— werewolves, hybrid vampires—I don't know, but whatever they are, I'm gonna kill 'em. I was really into that girl. So much, I was thinking about turning her so we could spend eternity together."

"That's surprising. Never thought of you as the type to settle down."

Chaos shrugged. "Sophia's not the jealous type; that's why we get along so well."

"I see," Elson said. "So what's going on with Sophia now? Is she outside on the loose—like all the others that have been bitten?"

"Nah, I got her chained up at my crib. For her own safety. She's shot out—crazy! And I think the combination of my saliva mixed with the infection from that bite wound has worsened her condition." Chaos closed his eyes sorrowfully. "I need some advice, man."

Elson leaned forward.

"Do you think Sophia will change back to her normal self if I go home and turn her?"

"It's doubtful, Chaos. She's likely to have the same mentality that she has right now. Believe me; you have to be careful about who you turn. Turning the wrong one can feel like a life sentence. Take Adelaide, for example. I found her in a mental institution in the early nineteen hundreds. Never meant to turn her, but I was nearly starved. Unable to quench my thirst, my lips lingered too long, and I've been stuck with her ever since. As you know, she recently turned a toddler. Now I not only have a crazy vampire under my roof, but I'm grandfather to a child that will never outgrow his terrible twos." Elson groaned and shook his head.

"That sucks, man. Adelaide's insanity can be too much to put up with sometimes. I'm over the top, but as wild as I am, I'm in control of my mental faculties. I can only tolerate Adelaide in small doses, and only when I'm high."

"You should try dealing with her and the kid at the same time. They give me a headache, and there's no peace in this house when they're around. To maintain my sanity, I had to kick them out of the mansion, and put them up in the guest house," Elson confessed, frowning in displeasure. "But, back to our current situation." He turned beseeching eyes upon Chaos. "Man, we're at war, and you're going to have to forget about your personal problems while we take out the creatures that are robbing us of our daily sustenance."

"Okay, I got you. What's the plan?" Chaos asked.

"We're only aware of one method that kills them; and that's severing their heads. We've decided to use our humans as bait to take out the flesh eaters in large groups when they swoop down on the fresh meat," Ismene informed.

Chaos nodded. "Good strategy."

Elson took a sip of blood, allowing the chilled liquid to saturate his mouth before releasing it to his parched throat. "But we have a problem…our stash of humans has dwindled significantly. We could use more warm bodies."

"I can't help you with that; I don't keep more than one or two humans on hand, and I'm traveling lighter than ever these days," Chaos said.

"You have Sophia," Ismene reminded.

"Nah, she's too close; I can't do that to her."

Elson made a scoffing sound. "You're not thinking rationally, Chaos. I want you to listen to me carefully."

Chaos looked Elson in the eye.

"Aside from Adelaide and her kid, my large and close-knit family was chosen very carefully. Times like now, their various specialties come in handy. Though close friends, you and I are very different. You don't want the responsibility of caring for a large group; you have always avoided close attachments, and under normal circumstances, I can respect that. But times like now, it would behoove you to join ranks with us, and give me your full support."

"That's what I'm doing, man," Chaos said irritably.

Elson's eyes briefly turned to slits. "No, you're not. I'm asking you to sacrifice Sophia—for the good of the group—for our survival. Why after all these years, do you want to finally start a family with someone who could be worse off than Adelaide?"

"But she might get better after she's turned."

"Her mind is gone and she'll never be the same. We're fighting to survive and you should do your part."

"I'll think about it…end of subject," Chaos said firmly. "So, what do you need me to do tonight?"

Elson let out a sigh. "Get your boys together and go out with Travis's team and study how they slaughter large numbers of those flesh-eaters. Once you've gotten the hang of it, you and your team should spread out to other areas. Hang their heads in visible places. I want everyone to know that we're at war."

Chaos rose to his feet. "You got it."

CHAPTER 28

The headaches were so debilitating, Jonas hadn't left his hotel room for days, nor had he accepted any of Holland's calls. He couldn't. It was unbearable to feel sound vibrations traveling through his ear canal. And his eyes had become so sensitive to light, he stayed inside his darkened, silent room, huddled in a chair and holding his head.

At first he thought he was imagining things when the shouts inside his head became intermingled with shrieks and screams that seemed to be coming from the corridor outside his room. *Why is everyone shouting?* Jonas wondered, bent over in pain as he made his way to his hotel door. Cracking open the door, he peered out to investigate. The bright light in the hallway caused his vision to blur momentarily, and when the scene in the hallway finally came into focus, Jonas was sure his mind was playing tricks on him.

At the far end of the corridor, two housekeepers were tussling and swatting at each other as they muttered curse words and called each other derogatory names.

"Hey! What's going on?" Jonas called out, careful to keep the volume of his voice down. But even the low tone caused him agonizing pain, and he dared not shout for fear of splitting his head in two. One woman picked up a bottle of cleaning product and threw it, hitting the other housekeeper squarely in the chest.

Incensed, the housekeeper who'd been hit with a bottle filled with green liquid, knocked over a cleaning cart, and leapt over the toppled vehicle with its tiny wheels spinning wildly. She was so enraged and so desperate for retribution, she seemed to soar in the air, with arms outstretched and fingers clawed as she sought out her opponent's throat. One on top of the other, both women squabbled on the floor. The one that seemed eager to wrap her hands around the other's neck was holding her victim down, and even from a distance of sixty feet, Jonas could see the woman's eyes burning with hunger.

Jonas raced along the corridor. Dismissing the pain in his head, he yelled for the two women to stop, and by the time he reached them, the one on top had used her teeth to rip into the other's throat. With a gouged-out eye and a throat that had been torn to shreds, the woman on the bottom was obviously dead. The other shouted what sounded like a war cry and launched into a macabre, victory dance, and then darted for the stairs.

Why hadn't these women responded to his call? Were they a new breed of creatures that didn't answer to any master? Confused, he followed the fresh blood scent that led down several flights of stairs and ended in the lobby. He heard a melee of screams, whining, and shouting, and braced himself before opening the door.

But nothing could have prepared him for the sight he beheld. The pristine lobby was now a gruesome crime scene with blood spatters covering walls, the marble floor, even the chandelier dripped blood. Bodies were sprawled in every direction. Jonas winced when he saw that the kindly receptionist's face had been eaten away.

On the lobby level, he ran from one end to the other, checking for survivors, but found only mutilated bodies in the gift shop, the computer center, and the restaurant. Making his way to the fitness center, Jonas detected movement, and the buzzing sound of machinery filled the air. He did a double-take when he spotted two figures together on a moving treadmill. One was taking bites out of the other, grazing leisurely while the human prey was stock still from shock or most likely from death.

"Stop!" Jonas yelled hoarsely. The aggressor froze and looked toward the sound of Jonas's voice. Jonas noticed that he had the decayed appearance of the creatures he had locked away. Seeming to recognize Jonas as an authority figure, the decomposing creature stood up and tottered toward Jonas, making whining sounds as he lumbered toward him.

Relieved that he wasn't being met with any resistance, Jonas hastily led his progeny through the restaurant and to the kitchen in the rear. There was an abundance of raw meat in the fridge, and the creature greedily shoveled lamb chops and pork tenderloin into his blood-filled mouth. Jonas locked him inside the restaurant and went to search for others that were a part of him.

It troubled him that the housekeepers had refused to heed his warning. What caused them to behave so disobediently? Jonas wondered. Comparing the differences between the housekeepers and the creature he'd captured in the fitness center, he realized that the housekeepers had maintained human qualities and were still attempting to function at their jobs. The rotting creatures, however, had lost all their human abilities and seemed to only respond to the scent of blood and Jonas's presence.

When had they arrived in Frombleton? How many were there? Were they responsible for infecting the housekeepers' and passing on their penchant for the taste of human flesh and blood? There were so many baffling questions swirling around in his mind, but he couldn't waste any more time trying to come up with answers. He had to amass as many creatures as possible, get them off the streets for the safety of the residents of Frombleton.

Outside the hotel, the streets were teeming with the newly infected, that were prowling around and snapping their jaws in their eagerness to feed. Some chased cars; others broke windows of business establishments in an attempt to feast upon anything that moved. Jonas shouted at them in a booming, authoritative tone, but as if he were mute and invisible, none of the infected gave him as much as glance.

He watched helplessly as a suit-wearing businessman used a briefcase to bash a cyclist over the head, knocking him off his bicycle and rendering him helpless on the ground. The business-man and a horde of starving people descended on the cyclist, clawing at him and biting in a frenzy of madness.

A woman raced along the pavement, pushing a double stroller that was occupied by curly-headed, identical girls.

"No! No!" Jonas shouted, as he ran behind the salivating crowd. They swarmed around the mother and her children, descending upon them, and covering them completely. Jonas pulled the ravenous creatures off, flinging them one by one, as far as he could. But each snarling creature he removed was quickly replaced by several others. They kept coming, so many of them that he was helpless to save the family that was being assaulted and brutalized. Sickened, he backed away, covering his ears against the terrible screams of the mother and her innocent children.

He stared in horror at the bloody massacre that was taking place on the streets of Frombleton and choked back a sob. All he'd ever wanted was to get an education, and to become a member of the healing profession one day. But instead, he'd become a killer and had fathered a legion of monstrous flesh-eaters that were rapidly multiplying.

He'd always thought of himself as a decent person, and had refused to believe Mamba Mathilde when she had accused him of being wicked and beyond redemption. But she was right. Here on the streets of Frombleton, these unholy creatures he'd spawned were the evidence of his corrupt soul. Never in his wildest dreams could he have ever imagined himself capable of creating such contemptible beings. Never could he have envisioned the scenes from hell that were hideously unfolding before his very eyes.

After discovering that raw meat satisfied his and his progeny's cravings, he'd been so certain that there'd be no more needless bloodshed. But that wasn't the case—not with this new strain of creatures. They were ravenous for human flesh and were completely uncontrollable.

He thought of Holland and swallowed in fear. Was she all right or had his vile spawn destroyed her, too? He looked up at the dark sky and felt comforted in the knowledge that Holland was protected by the force field that surrounded her home. The force field was meant to keep out vampires, could it also protect her from this new breed of flesh-eating creatures?

Jonas closed his eyes and imagined Holland's face. Feeling her presence as clearly as if she were within arm's reach, he knew intuitively that no harm had come to her—that she was safe and sound. It saddened him to imagine her sorrow when she realized that her spells could not save him, and sadly, he had to ask one last favor of her.

CHAPTER 29

Hours had passed, and Holland and Phoebe had made little progress toward the armory. Taking back streets had slowed them down, but avoiding the flesh-eaters required stealth and patience. During their journey, they discovered that abandoned cars and empty buildings were the perfect breeding grounds for the undead. They'd survived several ambushes before realizing they were better off walking in the middle of the street, rather than sticking close to buildings and cars.

Alert for even the slightest sign of movement, Holland and Phoebe carefully resumed their trek to the armory.

"You told those people that took the police car to make sure they find some place to hide, yet we're out here roaming the streets, making ourselves vulnerable," Phoebe complained.

"They don't have access to a safe house...we do."

"Yeah, but I'd feel a lot better if I had a weapon of some kind. Geez, it's getting so dark, it would be comforting to have a flashlight or even the dim light of my cell phone."

Holland nodded in agreement, and then suddenly flinched when a shadow appeared on the wall of a three-story, stone house.

"Just a cat," Phoebe assured her. Holland released a breath and looked around warily. In this dangerous, new world, all shadows were suspect.

Attempting to release tension, Holland began chatting with

her mother. "I wasted my time packing that duffle bag. A lot of good it's doing us, laying on the back seat of the Saab." She sighed, wondering if Rebecca would freak out when she found out that The Book of Spells was inside her backpack. Taking her mind off the spell book, she said, "I feel lost without my cell phone, too. If I had it on me, I'd call Rebecca. Even with all these corpses walking around, I'm sure she'd come out and pick us up."

Phoebe scanned the ground and picked up a small rock. Holland covered her mouth to stifle a snicker.

"Hey, don't knock it." Phoebe held up the rock. "This worked for primitive man, and it's better than being trying to ward off those *things* empty-handed."

"You're absolutely right. Sorry for laughing." Following Phoebe's example, Holland found a jagged rock and balled her fist around it.

"Geez, I'm tired. And I'm starving," Phoebe complained.

"Me, too."

"I don't think I've walked this far since I was a teenager."

"I don't think I've ever walked this far," Holland said with soft laughter. "My feet are throbbing and I can't wait to soak them."

"I hope Rebecca and her friends have lots of food on hand. I could go for a hot roast beef sandwich with gravy or a big plate of spaghe—"

"Shh. I hear something," Holland whispered. Seconds later, a hulking figure seemed to appear out of thin air. Holland and Phoebe shrieked in fear as a man wearing mechanic's coveralls stumbled out of a darkened gas station. His arms were outstretched as he groped in hungry anticipation. Without thinking twice, Holland hurled the rock, hitting him squarely between the eyes. Surprisingly, the rock knocked the mechanic off his feet.

Holland and Phoebe took off running for about a half-block,

but when they realized that they weren't being chased, they slowed their pace and looked over their shoulders. To their utter surprise, the mechanic hadn't risen. He was stretched out on the ground, his body unmoving.

"Do you think he's dead?" Holland whispered.

"He's already dead, isn't he?"

"I mean, dead-dead? You know—like, forever dead?"

"Well, he hasn't gotten back up, and I don't think they have the mental capacity to play possum," Phoebe said.

"We should check and see if he's like…unconscious or if he's actually dead-dead."

"No! That's crazy—why should we do that?"

"Knowing that it's possible to kill those *things* would be useful information."

"I don't know, hon." Phoebe gnawed on her bottom lip and shook her head doubtfully.

Holland's eyes swept the ground, looking for a replacement rock, but she didn't see anything except tiny stones and pebbles. "Stay here, Mom. I'll be right back."

"No, don't you dare go near that terrible corpse."

"It can't outrun me. The only way they get us is by outnumbering us or by taking us by surprise. My guard is up, and if it blinks or twitches, I'll take off. I promise, Mom. I'll be fine."

"Here, take this," Phoebe said, handing Holland her rock.

Rock in hand, Holland crept toward the motionless mechanic. Standing over him, she held up the rock, prepared to smash his face if he so much as moved a muscle. But he didn't move. With her rock lodged in the center of his forehead, a bubbling gore oozed out and trickled down his dreadful face. Holland poked him in the side with the toe of her shoe, but the corpse remained still and lifeless.

Grimacing, she tugged on the rock that jutted out of the creature's head. She worked to retrieve her weapon, gagging and dry-heaving at the squishy sounds that emanated as she struggled to dislodge the rock. A final twist and it popped out, and Holland nearly vomited at the sight of the disgusting mixture of thickened blood and clumps of brains that oozed out of the hole in the creature's head.

Carrying the slimy, blood-covered rock, she trotted back to her mother. Phoebe took one look at the blood-slimed rock in Holland's hand and recoiled. "Throw that down; it might be contaminated."

Holland handed Phoebe the untarnished rock and then wiped the tainted one against her pant leg. "The corpse is dead, and whatever disease it had probably died with it."

"You don't know that."

"I know I need a weapon. And until I get something better, this will have to do."

Phoebe gave a sideline glance to the trail of blood that streaked the front of Holland's jeans.

"The good news is, we know how to kill them. Aim for their head and strike hard!" Pleased with herself, Holland smiled.

As they moved along, they came upon a sign that read: Flowers, Bulbs, and Shrub. "Hey, Mom! I bet there's some cool stuff in there to kill those corpses with."

"No, there isn't. That's a gardening shop. Let's just keep moving. There's no telling what's lurking inside."

"We can't rely on these rocks for protection. We'll be out of luck if we throw them and miss. We need something sturdy and with a sharp edge...like a shovel. I bet that store sells shovels."

"It's dark in there, hon, and we won't be able to see those *things* creeping up on us."

"Just stick close. You guard the back and I'll guard the front."

Holland tried the door handle. Finding the door unlocked, she pushed it open slowly. Phoebe shook her head ominously and then followed Holland inside. With their backs pressed together, they entered the shop. "Over there," Holland said, pointing to the gleaming metal that shone in the darkness.

"Grab one and let's get out of here. I can't see anything!"

As they inched closer, Holland almost squealed in delight. "They have pitchforks, too. We're really in luck."

They exited the store and once they were back on the street, Holland held up the new weapons. "Pitchfork or shovel?"

"Either one—it doesn't matter."

Holland kept the shovel and gave Phoebe the lighter pitchfork. "I guess we can toss these now," Phoebe said, unclenching the rock in her hand.

"Keep it. It'll come in handy, if only to briefly immobilize a corpse."

"This is stupid; I don't need a rock and a pitchfork."

"It's not stupid, Mom. Trust me, okay? If we have to, we'll hit 'em with the rock and jab 'em in the head with the pitchfork and shovel."

The two walked in silence for the next mile, their senses attuned for potential threats. But when nothing jumped at them from the shadows, Holland soon let down her guard, becoming engrossed in her thoughts of Jonas. An image of his face was imprinted on her mind like a poster-sized photograph. His expression was one of anguish. He appeared to be suffering and in immense pain. His lips moved, and he seemed to be saying, *Holland, I need to see you one last time. I don't want to leave without telling you goodbye.*

Holland let out a soft moan.

"Is something wrong, hon? Did you see something?"

She shook her head. "Just another cat. Ran through the bushes and scared me."

Phoebe looked at the street sign. "I think the armory is nearby. It's on the seven hundred block of Halpern Street and we're at the corner of Seventh and Garfield Avenue. It's time to get off these small streets and venture onto the main streets. Are you ready?"

Holland nodded, her mind on Jonas. *Holland! Holland!* She heard him shouting in her mind.

CHAPTER 30

Plaintive wails and pained shrieks were coming from every direction. He could hear shouts of agony from miles away. The entire city was being massacred and it was his fault.

A white van came to a stop and a group of people, two men and a woman, emerged and stood staring at the bloody mayhem that was occurring. They didn't appear afraid. In fact, from their expressions, they seemed mildly amused. What's wrong with them; why are they standing around risking their lives? Jonas wondered. None of the creatures seemed aware of the people from the van, which he found puzzling. Looking at them closely, he detected that they weren't quite human and the way their eyes zoomed in on him revealed that they knew that he was something other than human also.

The female in the bunch regarded Jonas for a moment and then smirked. He saw something familiar in her fiery eyes, and the cruel curve of her mouth reminded him of Zac. And that's when it occurred to him that the people standing outside the van were vampires.

One of the males slid open the side door and yanked out a man who was struggling and thrashing and yelling for mercy. The vampire shoved the man out into the street, and then folded his arms and calmly observed as a horde of flesh-eaters swooped down on the man.

Jonas had failed the mother and her twins, but he wouldn't fail again. On the top of the biting and growling throng was a creature wearing a security guard uniform. There was a gun strapped to its side. Jonas yanked the gun from the holster and began shooting the creatures, aiming for their heads.

The vampires hissed and arched their backs like cats as Jonas fired the weapon repeatedly.

The female vampire advanced toward Jonas, and grabbed his arm. "This doesn't concern you; mind your business."

"It does concern me," he said, tugging himself out of her clawed grasp. "These creatures are my spawn."

"*Your* spawn? Who are you?" she asked with a sneer.

"I'm Jonas Laroche."

The female vampire sniffed the air that surrounded Jonas. "I don't know who you are nor do I know *what* you are, but it really doesn't matter. Be on your way, Jonas Laroche; you're in over your head. We own the mayor and the police force; we vampires are running this town." She smiled wide, revealing her fangs.

Jonas's first instinct was to grab her and choke her, but at the moment the thought entered his mind, all six vampires shot him dirty looks. Like Zac, they could read minds, too. Strangling her wouldn't have done any good. Killing vampires was as difficult as killing his kind.

Gazing down at the havoc on the ground, it was apparent that the creatures attacking the man from the van had now tripled in numbers. There weren't enough bullets in the gun to make a difference. There was no way to save the poor man.

Bleak hopelessness engulfed him, and Jonas stumbled away. He had to warn Holland that the vampires and the creatures he'd sired were a double threat in Frombleton.

Taking long and swift strides, Jonas made his way to Holland's neighborhood within minutes. Chilling screams coming from various houses filled the air. Aged and decayed creatures that roamed the streets hesitated when Jonas approached, as if expecting him to stop and chastise them. But Jonas kept moving. The newer, rogue creatures that still possessed the fresh looks of the living kept up their quest for blood and didn't seem to notice Jonas at all.

It was like the apocalypse, and if this was what Mamba Mathilde had foreseen, then he couldn't blame her for banishing him from her home.

Though he didn't feel worthy of forgiveness, he formed his lips in prayer, asking for mercy.

Outside Holland's home, he quickly discovered that he couldn't penetrate the force field. "Holland," he yelled. Cupping his hands around his mouth, he called her again. But his cries were met with a deafening silence.

Her house was dark and silent, and even more unsettling, he couldn't detect her powerful fragrance. What did that mean? Had she been attacked and murdered while he sat in his hotel room, tending to a headache? It was unfathomable that he had forsaken the one bright light in his life. He'd failed the one person who had loved him despite his unforgiveable flaws.

There was nothing else to live for if Holland was gone. And if she were still alive, she'd have a better life without the likes of him.

Trudging to the woods, Jonas knew what had to be done. In the moonlight, he moved low-hanging branches out of the way as he trekked with surefooted certainty toward the place where he'd once been buried. The area was covered with dead leaves and brush, but he recognized it as surely as he'd recognize his beloved former home in Haiti.

He brushed aside the twigs and leaves and began digging into the dirt with his hands. As he dug his own grave, he drew in a tortured breath, and a strangled sob tore from his throat.

⊕ ⊕ ⊕

At last, they were outside the armory. "We made it, hon; we made it!" Phoebe dropped the pitchfork and threw her arms around Holland. Holland squeezed her mother hard and then released her.

She lay her shovel down and reached out, attempting to penetrate the force field. She shot her mother a look of shock. "I can't get through."

"Yell for Rebecca or send her some sort of mental message. If she knows we're out here, she'll remove the barrier, won't she?"

"I don't think she can."

"What do you mean?"

"This is the work of numerous witches and it'll probably take an elaborate ceremony to take it down."

Phoebe looked over her shoulder, and in the distance she could hear the blood-curdling screams of people being attacked. "We've got to get in there before those *things* get close."

"I know. Give me a minute." Holland closed her eyes, trying to concentrate, but the sound of Jonas's voice was blocking her. *Please Jonas, I've got to help Mom. Please be quiet for a minute.*

As if responding to her plea, she heard Jonas say, "Goodbye, Holland," and then his voice went silent.

Too bad she didn't have The Book of Spells on her. That book could surely provide the right ritual to get through the force field. Times like now, she had to rely on her natural-born instincts and powers. With her eyes shut, Holland imagined herself pulling back bars of steel, and after a few moments, her fingers began to tingle. Arms outstretched and her hands curled around imaginary bars, she said, "Come on, Mom. I've got it open."

"I don't see anything. Which way should I go?" Phoebe asked anxiously. "And why are you sweating, hon?"

"Because…keeping these bars open is really hard."

Phoebe looked around with an expression of bafflement. "What bars? I don't see anything."

"Mom! Stop asking questions. Just step through the space between my arms," Holland said, panting and perspiring profusely as she struggled to keep the steel bars separated.

Phoebe squeezed sideways through the opening between Holland's arms and a sudden, bright smile flashed across her face. "You did it! I'm inside." She motioned for Holland to follow her. "Step inside, hon, and let the bars go."

"I'm sorry, Mom; I can't go with you." Holland released the bars and jumped backward.

"Why, Holland, why?" Phoebe ran toward Holland but was met with an electric-like wall of resistance.

The door to the armory opened and Rebecca came out. "Where are you going, Holland?"

"Take care of Mom; I'll be back." Holland knelt down and picked up the shovel.

"Please don't go back out there to fight those *things*. We made it, Holland; don't go back," Phoebe pleaded.

"I have to," Holland said, and held up a hand and waved good-bye.

Several women that Holland didn't recognize came out and ushered a sobbing Phoebe toward the door, and once her mother was safely inside, Holland walked off into the night.

CHAPTER 31

Holland no longer jumped at shadows; she didn't look over her shoulder every few minutes. Although her heart was heavy with the knowledge that something was terribly wrong with Jonas, she walked through the darkness, carrying a shovel, and feeling invincible.

There's something about love that removes fear, and Holland moved along the dangerous streets with Jonas's love wrapped around her like a cloak of protection.

She turned left and then right and then walked straight for several miles. She had no idea where she was going, but her feet seemed to move on their own accord, guiding her with the accuracy of a navigation system.

The chaos happening in the streets seemed to be happening in a separate reality. Holland bypassed graveyards of abandoned cars without incident. She walked close to new and crumbling buildings without terror. Nothing could stop her from heeding Jonas's call.

Finding herself in Naomi's old neighborhood, Holland paused and gazed at Naomi's house. *You were such a good friend, and I miss you. I hope you're in a better place, Naomi. Wherever you are has got to be better than being here.* She wiped a tear and continued until she ended up on the path that she used to take as shortcut home after leaving Naomi's house.

The path where she'd found the strange markings that she later discovered were Jonas's footprints. As if listening to the computerized voice of a GPS, she veered off the path and worked her way into the dark woods.

But the sudden blast of a gunshot caused her heart to leap in her chest and her feet to become frozen in place. The voice in her head was no longer guiding her. She was on her own and had no idea of which way to turn. She didn't know what she'd do if someone had hurt Jonas.

"Jonas, where are you?" she hollered. Her heart thumped so loudly, she doubted if she'd be able to hear anything if it didn't quiet down. Willing herself to move, Holland began running, her shoes crunching twigs and dried leaves. Small animals scurried from her path as she blazed a trail and finally stood a few feet away from Jonas's prone body.

"Oh, God. Jonas," she whimpered, her hand covering her mouth. She dropped the shovel and ran to him. Flat on his back with his arms outstretched, blood trickled from a hole in the front of his shirt.

"Who did this to you, Jonas?" Holland asked, lifting his head.

"I did," he gasped.

Holland gawked at the gun on the ground beside him. "Why, Jonas?"

"This is where it began, and this is where it has to end," he murmured. "My death is the only hope."

"No! I was working on another spell. I only need a few more days. My spell will set you free."

"It's no use. Too many of them. Those creatures will die with me." Jonas lifted his head and attempted to sit up.

"Don't move. Be still."

"I have to rest."

"Rest right here—in my arms."

Jonas dropped his head. "The vampires have grown powerful. They have people working for them in city government and on the police force. You have to use your magic on them."

"Okay. I will. But I need you to stay with me. Oh, Jonas, please don't die."

"I have to," he uttered and then forced himself out of her arms, groaning as he rolled away from her.

"Where are you trying to go?" she cried.

"Back to my burial place. To the most blissful sleep I've ever known. No more nightmares. No more voices or screams. Only sweet serenity." He coughed and took a shuddering breath.

"Jonas, don't go," she cried, reaching beneath his shirt and trying to stop the flow of blood with her hand.

"I'll always love you, Holland, but my time has come."

"No!"

"Yes! You must do something for me."

"What is it?" she asked in a voice that cracked.

"Cover my body with earth. It's the only way I'll find the peace I seek." With a painful grunt, Jonas flung himself away from Holland. A splash of moonlight revealed that he'd thrown himself into a deep hole in the ground.

At first, Holland shivered with horror at the sight of Jonas's crumpled body lying inside his self-made grave. Kneeling, she looked down at his lifeless form; weeping openly, she called his name. After what seemed like an eternity of shedding tears, she wiped her eyes, rose to her feet, and picked up the shovel.

Fresh tears sprang to her eyes when she heard the first batch of dirt hit his body. Sobbing mournfully, Holland shoveled dirt onto Jonas until his grave was completely filled.

CHAPTER 32

"**Y**ou did what you had to," Gabe said, trying to comfort Eden. But it wasn't much consolation. Taking out random biters was one thing, but putting down a man she'd grown to know was disconcerting. It didn't help that Leroy was furious with her. He'd confiscated his weapon and accused her of being trigger-happy, refusing to believe that Tony had turned into a biter, despite Charlotte's corroboration of Eden's story, and despite the evidence of the infected wound that Tony had hidden from everyone.

At Leroy's insistence, Tony hadn't been burned like the others; he was buried in the back of the store. Leroy had delivered a passionate eulogy that was tinged with accusations directed at Eden, and after the last shovelful of dirt had been heaped on Tony's body, Leroy had turned to Eden and Gabe and said, "You have a tank full of gas now, so I guess you two should be on your way."

Gabe and Eden gazed at Leroy in surprise. "Yeah, well, uh, I guess there's no point in hanging around," Gabe commented uneasily. "How much we do we owe you for the food and lodging?"

"No charge," Leroy muttered.

"I want you to know that we've appreciated your hospitality, and we'll be out of your hair first thing in the morning," Eden said. "And um, we're going to have to purchase more diapers and formula for Jane."

"Fill up some bags with baby items, food, and beverages. Take whatever you need, and get going," Leroy said, and then folded his arms.

"You want us to leave, tonight?" Eden asked anxiously.

"Yeah, I think it's best if you left my premises right away," Leroy said adamantly and then turned to Charlotte. "I'll give you a lift home in the morning." Eyes filled with grief, he left the main room of the store and climbed the stairs wearily.

"I don't think you two should be traveling around out there at night. I'm going to go upstairs and have a talk with Leroy," Charlotte offered.

Eden shook her head. "That's okay, Charlotte. Leroy thinks I overreacted because he didn't witness what we saw. Don't worry about us; Gabe and I will be okay."

Eden placed Jane in her makeshift bassinette and began packing up baby supplies while Gabe put together some snacks to take on the road.

Pacing nervously and peering through the slats at the window every few minutes, it was Charlotte who spotted the group of biters shambling along in the darkness. The awkwardly moving pack was still some distance away, but as they drew nearer, she caught sight of something familiar: a light-colored shirt with one sleeve rolled at the elbow and the other sleeve had unraveled midway down his arm.

"Ohmigod; it's Chuck! He's with a pack of those *things*, and they're heading this way!" With a hand covering her mouth, Charlotte scurried away from the window.

Gabe and Eden exchanged a glance, and together they responded to the threat. Gabe cocked his rifle and Eden picked up the nail gun.

"Oh, Jesus! Chuck is one of them now!" Charlotte wailed hysterically and began to shake uncontrollably.

"Pull yourself together, Charlotte, and take Jane to the back," Eden said harshly.

Responding to Eden's tone that was as sharp as a slap to the face, Charlotte gathered Jane in her arms and rushed to the storage room.

"We got trouble, Leroy," Gabe shouted.

"How many are there?" Leroy grumbled as he scrambled down the stairs, gripping his gun.

Gabe squinted through the spaces between the boards. "It's so dark; it's hard to tell. I'd guess about nine or ten."

Leroy ran a nervous hand over his face. "We can handle 'em; can't we?"

"Be a lot easier if Eden had a real gun," Gabe said, glancing at the nail gun Eden held.

"Oh, hell, I can't keep running up and down the stairs," Leroy spat, looking at Eden sneeringly. "Go on upstairs and grab that pistol in my top bureau drawer. It's inside a cigar box."

Eden raced up the stairs while Gabe and Leroy positioned themselves at the windows, eyes focused on the deadly crowd that was slowly approaching. But while the two men had their eyes trained on the area directly outside the store, there was an explosion of shattering glass in the back, and Charlotte gave a loud whoop!

Eden galloped down the stairs, pistol in hand, and her index finger on the trigger. Eden, Gabe, and Leroy raced to the storage room and were momentarily stunned to see grayish-colored, rotting hands groping through the spaces between the steel grate.

Leroy began firing rapidly, sending bullets through decaying hands and arms.

"Stop shooting; you're wasting bullets," Eden yelled.

"Don't tell me what to do," Leroy spat. "I'll waste as many bullets as I want to get those dang creatures off my property!" Looking crazed with anger, Leroy took several more shots until a couple of clicks indicated he was out of ammunition.

While Leroy went behind the counter to get his box of ammunition, Eden led Charlotte and Jane out of harm's way, and pointed to the stairway. Nodding in understanding, Charlotte bolted up the stairs.

Suddenly, there was the sound of cracking wood and loud splintering. The creatures were ripping the planks of wood away from the window. Judging by the volume of the unholy sounds and the size of the silhouettes outside the windows, the group had doubled—perhaps tripled—surrounding the perimeter of the place, determined to find a way inside.

"Get away from here, you sons of bitches!" Seething, Leroy aimed at the middle window and began blasting away.

"You're losing it, man. You've got to get a grip," Gabe cautioned. Paying Gabe no mind, Leroy continued advancing, and firing bullets aimlessly.

Within minutes, the wood was stripped from the windows and it was an unbelievable sight when the biters began crashing through the glass. Seeing arms and legs, thrusting through the shattered openings, seemed surreal, and Eden froze. Hearing the shots from Gabe's rifle snapped her into action. While Leroy fired at anything moving, Eden and Gabe aimed for the creatures' heads. But there were so many of them, pouring into the store from every available opening, Eden, Gabe, and Leroy were terribly outnumbered.

"Where's the ammo for this gun?" Eden asked Leroy with desperation in her voice.

"Upstairs! On the shelf in the closet," Leroy answered, still firing, his wild aim causing bullets to strike walls and display cases.

"There's no time to reload," Gabe said, tossing Eden the nail gun. Gabe was out of bullets also. He grabbed the ax. Swinging upward, he hacked into the head of the thing that used to be Chuck.

Eden watched in horror as the wood that framed the windows splintered and shot out in different directions. With the larger opening available, a legion of flesh-eaters poured into the store. *There's so many of them*, she thought woefully. Backing away, she raised the nail gun with a trembling hand. Shooting one or two wouldn't make a difference. It was over, and as scenes of her short life played in her head, she toyed with the idea of aiming the nail gun at her own head. *But what about Jane? I can't let those things devour my baby.*

As Eden turned toward the stairs, Gabe yelled out her name. She heard the ripping sound of fabric as one of the creatures grabbed the back of her shirt and yanked her away from the stairs. The nail gun flew from her hand and clattered to the floor. The sound of Leroy's firing echoed loudly, but none of his bullets connected with the thing that had captured her.

Split seconds later, she was being pulled down and the thing toppled on top of her. She struggled, tried to throw it off of her, while also preparing for the searing pain of teeth tearing into her flesh. When nothing happened, she used all her strength to pull herself from beneath the creature that lay upon her like a ton of dead weight.

She scrambled to her feet and watched in amazement as the horde of biters suddenly stopped moving. It was as if someone had pushed pause. One after another, they began to drop, hitting the floor like fallen trees.

CHAPTER 33

odies littered the streets, giving Frombleton the appearance of a war-torn city. People were out in droves. Some were trying to retrieve their abandoned cars and others were searching for loved ones. Along with the innocents that had lost their lives, all the flesh-eaters were dead—they died last night at the precise moment that Jonas had taken his last breath.

It was nearly dawn when Holland found her way back to Edgemont Avenue. She gave a relieved sigh when she spotted her mother's Saab. Stepping over bodies, she hurriedly opened the door. In the back seat, she found her mother's purse and her backpack. After a quick search inside the backpack, her fingers caressed the soft fabric that was wrapped around The Book of Spells. *Thank you!* Holland took the book out and clutched it to her chest.

The key was still in the ignition, and she got behind the wheel and steered the car onto the pavement, moving slowly until she found a side street that wasn't cluttered with people and cars.

Driving in the direction of the armory, she passed city vehicles and police cars. On behalf of the vampires, the city employees began the work of cleaning up the city. Holland wondered if the residents of Frombleton would ever lead normal lives again.

She arrived at the armory and surprisingly, the force field was down. Inside the large and vacant building, she found her mother and Rebecca in a dusty cafeteria, sitting on folding chairs and quietly sipping a beverage from thermoses. Oddly, Phoebe was dressed in a caftan and on her head was a turban made of stretch fabric.

"Where's everyone else?" Holland asked.

"Holland! Thank God, you're back!" Phoebe sprang to her feet so quickly, she splashed tea on the front of the caftan.

"Good to see you, Holland. You had us all extremely worried," Rebecca said.

"Sorry. Had something important to care of."

"Something to do with Jonas?" Phoebe asked, cutting an eye at Rebecca.

Holland swallowed and nodded. She couldn't talk about Jonas. Not yet. She looked around the large room, and then eyed Phoebe. "Whose clothes are your wearing, and...um...what's on your head?"

"This belongs to Rebecca; she let me borrow one of her ceremonial outfits last night."

Rebecca nodded. "Your mom joined in our ritual. She has very strong and positive energy—natural witch abilities. We've decided to assist her in realizing her potential," Rebecca said with a smile. Phoebe, in turn, beamed with pride.

"That's great, Mom. You've always said that we're from a long line of witches." Holland glanced around the room. "Where's everyone?"

"We chanted nonstop for hours and now that the flesh-eaters have been destroyed, we felt it was safe for everyone to go home and go about their daily lives. Your mother and I were waiting for you, and now that you're here, I guess we should all go home and get some rest."

Holland parted her lips to protest, to tell Rebecca that it wasn't the chanting that destroyed the corpses. It was Jonas! But she kept it to herself. At the moment, it hurt to think of him, and she was certain that she'd start crying uncontrollably if she spoke his name aloud.

"Has school reopened?" Holland asked.

"We haven't heard anything, so I guess we can assume that they're still closed until further notice. I'm surprised you're in a hurry to get back to school," Rebecca said.

"I'm not. Just curious to find out if things will ever get back to normal."

Rebecca clasped Holland's hands. "Yes, life is going to get back to normal. Be patient. Listen, your mother and I were talking. I was telling her about a new member of our coven who's working with the vampires."

"Are you serious—there's a witch working with the vampires?"

"Yes. She was forced into the job and so we've decided to take full advantage of her position."

"What's the plan? Is she going to expose them to the sun while they're asleep?"

"No, but what she's prepared to do can't be done alone. I need you to do something for us...but I don't think you're going to like what I'm going to ask of you."

Holland cut an eye at her mother, and Phoebe dropped her gaze, guiltily. "Uh...why won't I like it?"

Rebecca gave Holland's hand a little squeeze. "What we need you to do is going to bring up some bad memories. But all I ask is that you trust me. I need you to believe that I'd never do anything to hurt you."

"I do trust you, Rebecca."

"Good." Rebecca released Holland's hands and stared into her eyes. "We need you—all the citizens of Frombleton need you. We're relying on you for our survival."

"Whoa, that's a lot to deal with," Holland said, touching her forehead as if to get her thoughts together. "What do I have to do?"

"Donate blood. We need large quantities of your blood."

"No, I can't go through that again," Holland objected. "I was traumatized after witnessing what my blood did to Naomi. And after those witches at Stoneham used my blood for their own deceitful purposes, I've developed...like...a phobia. Listen, I want to help and I'd be happy to add my energy to chants and other rituals, but I'm really not comfortable with anything that concerns my blood."

"It's the only way we can defeat the vampires, hon," Phoebe said in a pleading tone.

"No!"

"Holland," Rebecca said gently. "This town is at the mercy of vampires. You're our only hope to overthrow them. Please."

Thinking about Jonas's warning about the vampires, Holland grew pensive and finally nodded. "What exactly do you need me to do? Please don't say you want me to go into their nest and allow a group of them to attack me."

"No, nothing that dreadful. In fact, you won't have to be in physical contact with them at all."

"Okay," Holland said bravely.

CHAPTER 34

For the fourth day in a row, Bradley M. Jones arrived at the Chandler Mansion, formerly know as the Sherman Mansion, at five in the evening. The vampires would begin waking up in an hour, and it was his responsibility to make sure that the human staff had everything in order. He shook his head ruefully. After all the education he'd acquired and despite his successful law practice, here he was, playing the role of a lackey. His job title was Chief of Staff, though he regarded his position as nothing more than a glorified butler slash accountant.

He walked from room to room, examining the work of the housekeeping crew. The marble floors had been polished to a high shine and everything seemed to be in order. Realizing that Elson Chandler would notice even the tiniest speck of dust, Bradley ran a white-gloved hand along the gold-plated bannister, over tabletops, and picture frames. Satisfied that the cleaning staff had done their jobs efficiently, he pushed a button that would stream classical music throughout the mansion—something that Elson Chandler insisted was the perfect way to begin his evening on the right note.

Next, he checked the kitchen staff. Vera Wesley scrubbed pots and pans, her lips scrunched together in repugnance. Working for vampires was distasteful; no one wanted to be in the mansion but they didn't have a choice.

On the other side of the room, Ulysses Andrews wore a somber expression as he cut chunks of bread that would be provided, along with a bowl of homemade chicken soup, to the blood slaves that were housed in the basement of the mansion.

"Hurry along, Ulysses. Mr. Chandler wants them fed at five-thirty precisely," Bradley prompted. Ulysses nodded grimly, and then began filling crude metal bowls with soup. The head cook, Franklin Haddock, opened the oven door and peeked in on the rack of lamb and baby red potatoes that were part of the menu that was planned for Mr. Chandler's esteemed guests. Tonight was special; tonight Mr. Chandler would be wooing state officials.

In the dining room, Sharla and Gretchen, two attractive women in their late-twenties, clad in formal maid's attire, prepared the long, formal table that could accommodate up to eighteen guests. The centerpiece was a simplistic yet elegant bouquet of bright yellow orchids. The table was set with crystal glasses, silver utensils, and bone china from Tiffany & Co. Nothing but the best for Elson Chandler's family and guests.

With Beethoven's "Moonlight Sonata" playing in the background, Bradley took the stairs that led to his office that was situated beneath the basement in the sub-basement. He bypassed the basement level as quickly as possible, cringing at the whimpers and cries of the people that occupied cages like animals. These unfortunate humans were kept on the premises to provide warm blood for the vampires as well as other cruel pleasures.

Had Bradley not accepted the job offer, his own daughter, Tessa, would be among the flocks of human beings that were packed inside cages.

Adjourning to his office, Bradley sat in front of the computer. On the monitor, he checked the household expenses for the week, noting that Mr. Chandler paid less for the upkeep of this nineteen-thousand-square-foot residence than Bradley paid to keep his small law office afloat. The free labor that Mr. Chandler enjoyed was criminal. But it seemed there was nothing anyone could do. The vampires had staked their claim on the town of Frombleton and though it was unlawful, the citizens went along like sheep, terrified of the consequences if they objected or voiced a complaint with state-level government officials.

And now that it appeared that Mr. Chandler would soon have state officials under his thumb, the future of the entire state looked glum.

There was a soft knock on Bradley's office door. He glanced at the clock. Too early for the vampires to be pestering him, he noted with relief. "Come in," he said, expecting to see Ulysses or one of the maids. He was pleasantly surprised to see Tanya Fluegfelder; her mass of red hair, pert nose, and pretty face were a delight to the eyes. It was a shame that she, too, had been forced into servitude to these ungodly creatures.

"Good evening, Tanya," Bradley said, unable to keep a smile off his lips. He rarely saw Tanya. She had an office on the second floor in Mr. Chandler's vast library—organizing his books, Bradley had assumed. She performed other services for the vampires, but Bradley wasn't exactly sure what her duties entailed. He'd heard a rumor that she was romantically involved with that cowboy, Travis. Feeling a stab of jealousy, Bradley wondered if Tanya's feelings for the vampire were sincere.

"Nice music," Tanya said, referring to a Mozart piece that was now playing.

"Mr. Chandler has good taste in music."

"His library is rather extraordinary also. The Frombleton Library pales in comparison to his extensive collection of rare books." Tanya toyed nervously with her fingers. "But...I didn't come down here to talk about books; I need to ask you a favor."

"What can I do for you?"

"I'm invited to Mr. Chandler's dinner party, and I need to go home and change…" Tanya paused and looked away embarrassedly.

"That's not a problem as long as you're finished categorizing your books or whatever it is you do on the second floor."

"My librarian duties are complete."

"Well, then run along and glamour yourself up—not that you need much help in the beauty department." Bradley sighed inside. Tanya was too lovely and demure to be involved with that crude cowboy. He wondered if they were intimate…sexually. He frowned at the thought.

"I usually serve the chilled blood to the vampires when they rise, and I was wondering if someone else could do that tonight. All they have to do is carry the blood trays up to the second floor and leave them on the table near the top of the landing. The vampires come out and help themselves, and Ismene personally serves Mr. Chandler."

"Then I'll send Sharla and Gretchen upstairs with the trays."

"Thank you. The glasses have already been filled, and the trays are in the fridge."

"Very well. I'll pass on the information."

"Thanks, Mr. Jones."

"Call me Bradley. Please."

"Thank you, Bradley," Tanya said and produced a smile that reminded Bradley of flowers and sunshine and all that was still good in a world that would soon be dominated by vampires.

⊕ ⊕ ⊕

Despite the lighting in his office, the room became dim when the sun went down. Bradley inhaled deeply. Mr. Chandler would want to confer with him before he was allowed to leave for the evening. Working in this house was like being sentenced to work for the devil in hell. Although lovely music flowed into every room, in a short while there would be pitiful shrieks overwhelming the tinkling piano keys.

That crazy vampire, Adelaide, and her monster-child refused to drink chilled blood. It was Rufus, the security guard's, responsibility to select a human from the cages and take the ill-fated person to the guest house, where the famished vampire woman and child would feed until the unfortunate human was completely drained.

Being that Mr. Chandler didn't want any vampires roaming around that were sired by crazy Adelaide, it was also Rufus's responsibility to drive a stake through the human's heart before he or she turned.

Wishing that his office was high on the third floor, Bradley braced himself for the screams that were apt to vibrate the floor beneath his feet. He prayed that Rufus would work quickly, and get the poor soul over to the guest house without delay.

CHAPTER 35

The vampires awakened one-by-one and emerged from their various rooms, rubbing their eyes, gliding toward the scent of blood while still clad in sleeping attire.

"Mmm. Smells delicious," Florencia said as she reached for a glass filled with rich, red blood.

Travis moved in front of Florencia. "I say ladies before gents, but I'm feeling extra thirsty and that blood has a divine scent."

Sniffing the air, four more vampires convened around the tray, but no one took a swallow. No one was allowed to drink until Elson had downed his first glass of blood of the evening.

Moments later, Ismene glided down the hall, wearing a beautiful silk negligee with a lace bodice. She was carrying two glasses: one for her and the other for Elson.

Clutching their glasses, the Chandler vampires padded back to their side of the mansion, prepared to guzzle their wonderfully fragrant blood rationing at the appointed time of six-ten.

⊕ ⊕ ⊕

Travis stumbled out of his room, holding a hand to his chest. "I'm burning inside," he gasped. "Elson, don't drink the blood. We've all been poisoned!"

Smoke seeped from the pores of Lisette's body. A fountain of blood bubbled inside Florencia's mouth. Out of their minds from the unbearable, scorching pain, the sisters joined hands and flung themselves out of a second-floor window.

Torturous shrieks and sounds of frenzied clawing echoed throughout the mansion immediately after the vampires ingested the lethal blood. Howling male voices beneath the high-pitched shrieks of the females created an unholy cacophony of sound.

Hearing the unearthly commotion, the staff was too afraid to go upstairs and investigate, and one by one, they began exiting the mansion and running for their cars.

By the time Rufus returned from the guest house, Bradley was waiting for him at the servant's entrance.

"What's causing all that commotion?" Rufus asked.

"I think they're all dying."

"Who's dying?"

"The vampires," Bradley replied, eyes large with astonishment. "Poisoned blood. You need to unlock those cages. Let those people out."

"But…suppose Mr. Chandler is okay. Suppose only the others drank the poisonous blood."

"Let them out," Bradley insisted.

The ding of the elevator caused both Bradley and Rufus to jump. "It's Mr. Chandler. I know it is, and he's gonna kill us," Rufus said, eyes bulging in fear.

Bradley snatched the key ring that was hanging out of Rufus's pocket and began unlocking the cages, letting out people, many of whom he knew from around town.

The caged people escaped through every available exit, and ran barefoot through the night.

Upstairs on the main level, the elevator doors were open. Bradley and Rufus crept toward the open doors and flinched at what they saw. On the floor, Ismene was curled in the fetal position, writhing in agony, and surrounded by a puddle of brownish liquid. "Help me," she gasped, reaching out an arm.

Bradley's blood instantly turned to ice when he realized that the skin on Ismene's arm was dripping onto her nightgown, and she was lying in a pool of her own melted flesh.

"Dear God!" Rufus cried and covered his face with his hands.

"Where's Mr. Chandler?" Bradley asked, injecting false concern in his voice.

"Dying. My great father is upstairs dying; he needs help."

"We'll help him," Bradley said. He whispered to Rufus. "Where's your stake?"

"I left it in the guest house."

"Do you have any others?"

"Yeah, I keep them in the pantry."

"Get one. Hurry," Bradley ordered.

Rufus returned with the wooden stake. Glancing into the elevator, he could see that there was nothing left of Ismene except a sickly, liquid substance. Even her silk and lace negligee had crumpled into ashes.

Bradley took the stairs to Elson's wing. He had to know for sure that his and Tessa's tormentor was actually dead. At the top of the landing, there was Elson, clutching his chest but very much alive. In an angry, sweeping gesture, Elson knocked the remaining glasses of tainted blood off the table.

"I only took one sip of that poison," Elson rasped with blood trickling down the side of his mouth. "Bring me a human from one of the cages. All I need is fresh, warm blood and I'll be all right."

Bradley was so shocked to find Elson alive and pretty much intact, all he could do was gawk at the vampire.

"Did you hear what I said. Bring me a live human!"

Bradley's head nodded involuntarily, as if someone was controlling him like a marionette.

"Go!" Elson bellowed.

Suddenly, Bradley whipped the stake out that he'd been hiding behind his back. Elson hissed like a rattler and lashed out, raking his long fingernails across Bradley's face. Still possessing his superior vampire strength, Elson flung Bradley, sending him crashing into a wall. Bradley slid down to the floor and noticed a wineglass that was only missing the stem. Inside the cupped portion was a sufficient amount of blood.

Bradley prayed that his plan would work. Panting, Elson leaned against a wall, gathering his strength. Cup in one hand and the wooden stake in the other, Bradley rushed toward the ailing vampire and flung the contents of blood in his face.

Elson's hands went up to his face and he went silent—from shock, Bradley surmised. Then he pulled his hands away, revealing that his face had completely melted away. Smoke wafted from the holes where his eyes, nose, and mouth used to be.

With Elson reeling in unimaginable pain, Bradley ran toward him and drove the stake through his heart.

CHAPTER 36

There was no explanation for how all the biters had dropped dead at the same time, but Eden was eternally grateful to have a second chance. True to his word, Leroy drove Charlotte home. Charlotte still hadn't been able to get in touch with any of her family or friends; they had no way of knowing if the plague had hit Charlotte's home town. Eden didn't envy the task that lay ahead for Charlotte. The poor thing had lost her fiancé and had possibly lost her entire family.

"Do you still want to head for New York or would you like to give Willow Hills another chance? You can stay at my place for as long as you want," Gabe said as he steered the Explorer, weaving around the dead bodies that cluttered the streets.

"I don't know if that would work. I'm not giving up Jane, and I don't want us to be a burden to you," Eden murmured, looking down at the baby that cooed in her arms.

"You two could never be a burden. Don't forget, I care about Jane, too. And I also care about you."

"I want to…but I'm not sure if it's a good idea. Suppose there's nothing between us except the camaraderie of battling biters together."

"I could accept that. Look, no strings attached, Eden. No labels. We'll be roommates. Two people enjoying each other's company, while allowing the friendship we've developed to blossom into love…or not," he said with an adorable smile.

Eden laughed and gazed down at the baby. "What do you think, Jane?" When Jane gurgled loud and happily, Eden and Gabe burst into laughter.

⊕ ⊕ ⊕

Tires squealed as the white van tore down the road.

Chaos had always planned on visiting New York, but he'd never imagined making the journey with crazy Adelaide and a demanding two-year-old vampire child. He sighed in resignation. Elson Chandler had been a good friend for over a century, and looking after what was left of Elson's family was the least he could do.

Chaos gave a groan when Adelaide turned up the volume of the radio and began singing a completely different song than the one pouring from the speakers. The little boy began shouting for blood, but Adelaide kept singing.

Unable to bear the racket any longer, Chaos pulled to the side of the road. In the back of the van, he popped the lid of the cooler. Before retrieving the packet of blood, he gazed at the twisting and writhing woman that was bound by chains. "As soon as we get where we're going, I'm going to turn you, Sophia, and we're going to be a family."

Back in the car, he gave the packet to the screaming child, and was relieved when the yelling stopped. Two minutes later, the boy was screaming for more.

"Is he gonna take a nap any time soon?" Chaos asked Adelaide with irritation coating every word.

"He sleeps when we do…at dawn," she said in a sassy tone and resumed her loud singing.

Back behind the wheel, Chaos revved the engine, and shook his head. *Rest in peace, Elson. Should we ever meet again, you best believe, you owe me one!*

⊕ ⊕ ⊕

Rebecca and her coven sisters hailed Holland as a hero, but in Holland's mind, the real heroine was Tanya Fluegfelder. All Holland had had to do was endure the prick of a needle. What Tanya had done, making sure that the vampires were served Holland's vampire-killing blood, took true courage.

Now that Phoebe had been accepted into the coven, she seemed to have a new sense of purpose, and for the first time since Holland's dad had died, Phoebe seemed truly happy.

The area of Jonas's burial site was covered with leaves and brush, yet Holland knew the exact location instinctively. Kneeling, she placed purple mums and cream dahlia upon his resting place, and then stood up and admired the bouquet.

"I hope you like the flowers. I thought the colors seemed masculine," she said in a conversational tone, as if Jonas was standing next to her. "The town is back to normal, and you'd never know that Frombleton had been overrun with flesh eaters and vampires. I've heard rumors that a few vampires escaped, but no one knows for certain..." Holland paused as if listening to Jonas's response.

"Mom is in Rebecca's coven; isn't that cool? The coven sisters are going to stay alert for any vampires, but I doubt if a vampire would be foolish enough to return to Frombleton." Holland gave a long sigh. "There's something I have to tell you. I'm going back to Stoneham. I miss those cool, witch classes, and all I'm doing at Frombleton High is daydreaming and thinking about you."

She paused and rearranged the flowers. "I got these flowers at the grocery store. They didn't cost much, but it's the thought that counts, right? Anyway, I won't be visiting you for a while. I won't be home again until summer break."

Holland pushed herself to her feet. "I'm gonna miss our conversations, Jonas. And please don't forget how much I love you."

I love you, too! Holland heard Jonas say. And she smiled and blew him a kiss.

Joelle Sterling lives in Philadelphia, PA. She is the author of *The Dark Hunger* and *Midnight Cravings*. Contact the author at Joellesterling3@aol.com